MAYBE

Previous Books by Burt Blechman

THE WAR OF CAMP OMONGO

HOW MUCH?

STATIONS

THE OCTOPUS PAPERS

MAYBE

A Novel

Burt Blechman

Prentice-Hall, Inc., Englewood Cliffs, N.J.

for

Anita, Gladys, and Miss Moore

MAYBE

Daylight Saving Time

⌒

. . . maybe, Myra decides. Maybe the biggest problem in life is how to spend it. Next, without doubt, is happiness. Last, and worst of all, money. And where to find it.

For the hundredth time, she's ransacked her mind for the clue. Tomorrow she'll start on the master bedroom. A hidden floorboard, a drawer with some cunning and devilish compartment. Buried doubloons, gold from the Spanish Main, handsome pieces of eight—a pleasant moment of possibilities as she thumbs through the heavy volume. *Famous Last Words,* indeed. As if it's there, in the rental library, a solution to her husband's deathbed puzzle. *"I regret that I have but one life to give to my country."* For a patriot, no sacrifice is too great. *"Don't shoot till you see . . ."*

A frantic cannonade from the kitchen.

"Rose," she cries out. "Anything wrong?"

Sounds of crockery being swept into a dustpan. Her precious setting for twelve, the Apostle Pattern, one by one being crucified. When Ralph passed away, there were still eight. Now she's down to three. Soon there'll be two, then one. Her own. A remnant of past glory surrounded by Japanese imitations. If only she could restore it to the original dozen, walk into a department store and resurrect her disappearing dishes. But they're out-of-stock, outdated. Like her.

"If you need help, Rose, just ask!"

She mustn't get Rose upset. Maids are hard to find nowadays. As scarce as money, friends, happiness. And besides, dishes aren't everything.

Two shattered Apostles dive into the dustpan. "Don't nag," shouts Rose. "You only get upset."

Naturally she's upset. With the meeting canceled, her schedule is in a complete turmoil. Not so much a turmoil, just a void. An empty afternoon followed by a vacuous evening. It's advancing on her, breathing across her face with its chloroform breath—a lull, the deadliest problem of all.

If it were A.M., she'd bury herself in a spiritual get-together. But it's P.M., her duties with Divine Technology are over, and there's nothing to do but wait it out till Monday, just one dinner and a single sleepless night away.

Myra glances at her heavily-jeweled watch. Of course!

4

Daylight Saving. Sixty minutes killed, wasted, saved; it all depends on your outlook. Hurriedly she adjusts the time-piece.

"Rose, we've just lost an hour," she announces joyfully. "Set the clocks ahead, dear. The grandfather clock, the cuckoo clock, the alarm clock, the seven-day clock, the perpetual clock. . . . Thank goodness for Daylight Saving!"

"I'm busy, Mrs. Russell. Nailing back this loose floorboard you tore up."

As if Rose hasn't all the time in the world. But enough of Rose, the bewitching hour approaches. The gap between twilight and darkness. A torturous night lies ahead, she can sense it, awaiting her with the restless arms of a spurned, insatiable lover.

Mustn't touch! For a widow, those television machines can be as dangerous as X-rays, as damaging as drugs. And life is far too precious to waste on drugs when you're fifty-nine with so many tasks to be undone.

Myra plunges into her budgetary problems: a generous donation to CONTROL—had to in order to save face; a visit to her doctor—probably psychosomatic; household services for Rose—if only she could share Rose with another unfortunate widow; three fat checks for three fabulous boutiques—but you can't go to fund-raising meetings in rags; a modest handout to SANITY—and isn't the future of the world worth something, too?

No, it all comes under necessities. She can no more do without clothes or a hairdo or for that matter SANITY, than live without breathing. And if breathing is perfectly natural, life is outrageously costly. They're both axioms and an axiom can't be altered any more than one's age. Approaching sixty! Life slipping by with the force of an onrushing locomotive. Hurry, hurry, she must do something before it's too late.

❧

She'll sell a few more shares. It's that or dispose of Rose. Who's stuck with her through thick and thin, through war and peace, marriage and widowhood, through years of fascination and these awful, post-Ralphean times.

Myra hands the uniformed man a glittering coin. That frightful scowl. Because he's about to be replaced. A new aluminum elevator—buttons, batteries, electronics, progress. "Cheer up," she smiles. "Maybe they'll decide to keep you."

The gold-and-crimson attendant looks gloomier than ever. He's on his way out, too. Self-service elevators, do-it-yourself doors. The whole world growing progressively automatic. It can't be helped, she decides, handing the doomed doorman a piece of silver.

Myra Russell lifts herself into the gaily-colored cab. "Wall Street," she mutters with dismay.

They race down the gilded avenue, whizzing by glass-and-chrome towers, pausing at condemned and old-fashioned brownstones. About to disappear, like giraffes and bald eagles. Because there are too many creatures with too little planet. That frightening explosion of the earth's population. She can feel her blood pressure mounting. A grim world. But the way to improve it is to understand, propose, act. To engage in life, to be immersed in it like a drowning swimmer. Which means discussing current events with taxi drivers as well as domestics.

"Six children!" she repeats. "That's quite a family you have."

The cabbie grunts.

"I suppose, then, you've never heard of the population . . ."

The driver interrupts with a screeching brake. A hot radio bulletin. Million dollar trade. Baseball, football, hockey. That's right, hide your head in the sand like a silly old ostrich. The sports extra ends; the cabbie steps on his gas; the newscaster continues. "Bomb. Buildup. Crucial. Looks like . . ."

He switches to jazz. The cab lurches to a stop. Myra examines the driver's sad, Irish eyes. Six children. A crime. She hands him a tip, halfway between modest and extravagant. Now she's subsidizing large families. He smiles gratefully.

"Railroads are out," commands the broker. "Have you considered missiles?"

"Never!" her SANITY button glowing with indignation. "Ralph's friend swears the D&K Railroad will go up again. If Alex saw me nibbling away on my estate just to meet expenses, he'd burst a blood vessel."

How to survive on D&K's dividends? Of course she could survive, but living means more than mere survival. How much more, that's the grisly question.

"Sell just a few," Myra concludes. "I'm sticking with what I have, an established, reliable railroad. If it was good enough for my husband, it's good enough for me."

7

A flickering remembrance, how, on that day Ralph died, D&K took the fatal plunge. From 59 to 28½, now 15¾. But she's got to have faith in futures. She must believe in the possibility that it's hiding somewhere in her spacious apartment, those last words transformed into a bundle of cash as thick as her waistline, bound by a stout cord, tagged with a fond farewell: *This treasure is for my darling wife to see her through the bitter years. With the compliments of her departed husband, Ralph.*

"And no missiles. I'm not contributing one penny more than I háve to. And these days you have to. Every hairdo, every hit show, every taxi ride, all adding a few more bullets."

"I see," says the securities analyst, looking insecure.

Why try to convert people like that? People whose faith is in bombers, guns, despair. People whose faith in man is tax-exempt.

"Have you," continues the fretful little broker, "considered oils, Mrs. Russell?"

Myra conjures up a free-wheeling, oily Texan. And, on the other side of the tracks, the right side, a trustworthy train conductor.

"D&K," she decides. "Of course I could manage without selling. If I told my maid that after twenty years I don't need her. If I stopped playing canasta and going to decent restaurants and taking taxis. If I stayed home all day and did nothing, I wouldn't have to cash a single stock. I know it's wrong to spend my estate. But not everything wrong is bad. What's important is intention. And my intention is to keep finding worthwhile things to do. Sell. That's my final

8

intention. I am not going to sit home every day bored to tears. Just because I'm a widow," she looks at him grimly, "doesn't mean I'm dead."

Myra descends the crooked marble stairs. She told *him* a thing or two. If only Ralph could have seen. And Alex would have been proud as a peacock. Which species is rapidly being extinguished thanks to those American housing projects in New Guinea. Thanks to greed, graft and a higher standard of living. Which is fine, she's no reactionary, as long as it doesn't interfere with the freedom of orangutans, trumpeter swans and koolie birds.

A frightful world, with its dwindling game preserves, its shrinking zoos. Soon there won't even be pet shops. A friendly poodle is out of the question. It's not right buying affection. And it certainly wouldn't be fair to antagonize Rose after two decades of well-meaning servitude. She is not going to cut Rose's salary and that is that. If she has to, her back to the wall, her budget closing in, she'll simply start taking subways. And why not?

Why not save money for a change, preserve the remnants of her dwindling estate? Other people take the subway and "other people" means her as well. For the first time in centuries, Myra, her ermine bristling like a wary groundhog, descends into the bowels of the city. Who knows, maybe she'll even enjoy it.

Enjoy! It was monstrous, straight out of Dante. Herded like swine, pressed like ducks, humanity rushing toward a sardine-can destruction.

"No!"

The cab screeches to a halt.

"My ruby watch," shouts Mrs. Russell. "Ralph's farewell gift. Stolen!"

The blue-eyed driver shrugs.

"In the subway," she explains. "Snatched right off my wrist," holding it out. "Maybe," she concedes, "it fell off. A loose clip."

"A pickpocket," declares the cabbie. "Happens all the time."

"Horrible," says Myra, remembering how she canceled the insurance, how she's cut expenses, how she mustn't buy a jeweled replacement, cashing in more D&K's, which will mean fewer shares, smaller dividends, a diminished future. "I can't blame anyone but myself. It was plain, old-fashioned carelessness."

"Listen, lady, take a tip from someone who's been around. Keep away from them subways," as he guides her on a devious but fascinating route.

Myra, reflecting on the grim advice, rewards him with a generous tip. The doomed doorman welcomes her like a long lost (which indeed she was!) friend. Another reward. The about-to-be-replaced elevator man gives her an insipid smile. A third award. After all, in a few months they'll be totally unemployed, destitute, with nothing to do but stare at television and gobble tranquilizers.

A garish prospect.

❦

Odd Thursdays are taken care of by opera. Naturally, pressed for funds, she could sell her subscription, raise some ready cash. But how would she ever refill those empty odd evenings? Goodness knows the even ones are difficult enough.

The stately conductor enters, bows and lifts his baton. The magic curtain begins to rise. The fascinating chatter is stilled. A prolonged overture. The singers gaze dumbly, a conference of deaf mutes. They forgot their lines! No, she can hear the coach, hiding under the floorboards, barking out his cues.

What a fool not to have bought a libretto. Something to do, something to look at. But she has got to economize somewhere, and librettos are a good place to begin.

It sounds Italianish. She remembers how, after Ralph's death, she buried herself in grammar, syntax, *signor* and *signorina*. A dismal failure. Just couldn't concentrate. She should have taken French, the language of diplomats. Not that she isn't diplomatic. Even with Rose, who is so suppressed it's shameful. She ought to come right out with it: *Rose O'Connor, it happens that my railroad shares are descending, I don't have a cent of security and I've got to find it. The treasure, dear. The one poor Ralph tried to tell me about before his untimely* (what other kind is there?) *death*. But Rose would say no, she's got too much work turning on switches, defrosting dinners, supervising scrubwomen. Rose is right. You can't add treasure-hunting to the long list of domestic chores. It's strictly a personal problem. Which means she's got to keep it secret. Let Rose accidentally stumble on the treasure and the only decent thing would be a fifty-fifty split. Why split what hasn't even been found? Best to leave fate alone, leave Rose to her dusting, and let the treasure suddenly, like King Arthur's sword, emerge from the lower depths. Meanwhile, impoverished or not, she's in a world-famous opera house, the singers are shrieking their vocal troubles and there's no time like the present to sit back and figure out what's going on.

The gypsies are stirring. Or are they Venetian vagabonds? An elderly hag is humming, sometimes gloriously, sometimes woefully. Now she's forgotten the name of the opera. She'll have to light a match. She remembers the fire rule, the five-hundred-dollar fine, her promise to economize. Meanwhile, there's the opera, the stunning but endless opera.

The subscribers look like freshly slain corpses, the opera house, a gilded mortuary. A gigantic lull wraps the two thousand spectators in its dismal, tuneful shroud. She's got to replace her Apostles, mothproof her carpet, buy a new watch, discover the treasure, pay her phone bill. She's got to pay attention.

The Italian is incredulous. The singing, off-key. The acting, grotesque. The instruments pluck, scrape, quiver, wheeze, each in its own sour container.

The elderly gypsy, or is she a penniless dowager, steps to the center. The audience is still. A scattering of coughs, last breaths, dying oaths. From the balcony, a distant snore. Myra grips her velveteen seat. Dear Powers Above, don't let her slip away, her mind wandering, her patience overtaxed, her imagination spent. The hours—or are they minutes?— tick on relentlessly. Two thousand timepieces drowning the hall with horological opera buffa. If only she had a watch.

At least then she'd have something to look at, something to focus her attention.

She's about to become a widow! That's the husband, writhing across the stage with a knife in his back as he fortissimos his plea for revenge. Gypsy bitch, she killed her own husband! No, maybe it was just an accident. An unexpected suicide. The Romany dowager, smiling, laughing, trilling happily, is free at last to find a true lover.

The husband dies on a dismal note. The merry widow is alone. Outside, behind the Greek palace, you can hear the chorus of melodic rakes and cheerful libertines, soprano sweethearts and basso beaus: having wonderful time, wish you were here. But the widow chants a pianissimo of disillusionment, wondering what to do, where to turn, when to sing.

The invisible chorus dies away. The pianissimos lengthen. The lulls grow more ponderous. More snores, more yawns, more unintelligible Sicilian. A prolonged lullabye. On and on. Another opera down the drain. Another day is done. How many days till sixty? Till seventy, eighty? If only she had the courage to rise indignantly from her seat, to step over the sleeping subscribers, never again to return.

But what would she do then with her Thursdays, those worthwhile, educational, unbelievably odd Thursdays?

❧

"CONTROL or Die!" roars the speaker, "a phrase that'll catch their attention." The women nod attentively, whispering, filing fingernails, combing hair, applying lipstick, occasionally listening. Myra is a listener. That's why she prefers front rows. So she won't be diverted by their wasteful gossip, their expensive millinery, their mannered indifference.

The director of public relations continues his impassioned solo. "There's nothing abnormal, ladies, about the birthrate. It's the death rate that's out of whack. If only there were a drug-resistant virus, a mysterious and incurable disease, it'd solve the population explosion in a jiffy."

Refusing to listen to her neighbor's recipe for cherries *flambé*—did she say brandy or bourbon?—Myra nods her brunette head in complete agreement.

"Not a famine, which is awkward, but an epidemic. Something painless, humane, and deadly."

Mrs. Benedikt raises her pudgy hand. It doesn't seem right to wear that many diamonds. Not when they're discussing problems as grim as famine and birth control. Goodness knows she does her share, dieting the way she sometimes does. And if everyone had just one son, there'd be no overcrowding, no explosion, no CONTROL. Then where would she spend her Tuesday evenings?

"Scandalous," pronounces Mrs. Benedikt, her diamonds jingling against her breasts, "turning CONTROL into a sounding board for sheer rabble-rousing. A matter as delicate as birth should not be for street-corner discussion. Let me make a suggestion: why not purchase a fine mailing list from the Museum of Modern Art or *Harper's Bazaar*? Then we could send out a discreet and well-designed announcement."

Swank, even their mailings. The things she had to do to join CONTROL. All those references. And that initiation

14

fee, three whole shares way back when it was over 20. But well worth it. It's so different from the others. Each has its own benefits. CONTROL she enjoys because it's so classy, SANITY because it's so urgent, CHEMBAN because it's so scientific, and CONSERVE because it falls on Wednesdays.

The discussion takes a turn for the worse. A heavyset gynecologist. Looks as if he's pregnant, milk-filled breasts and all. The women stir uneasily. Coughs. Whispers. Myra senses a lull. This is no joking matter. CONTROL *or Die*. She grips the edge of her chair, forcing herself to seem intrigued.

"We come to the main problem: which brand to purchase for our pilot program in Rangoon. *Stallions* are less elastic but more durable. *Arab Chiefs* are less costly but more pleasureful . . ."

She'll cast her ballot for *Arab Chiefs*. An enticing name. Anyhow, the doctor with big breasts says it's more pleasurable. And cheaper, too. Yes, she'll vote for the cheapest, the Arabs.

"Discussion tabled!"

Thank the Lord. There's one thing she can't stand, and that's technicalities.

"I want to congratulate you, ladies," smiles Mrs. Benedikt, "for seeing us through this frightful labyrinth of contraception. We'll take the matter up at a future date when we can find more time. Now for the important business of the day, the name of our *dansant*."

The meeting comes to life. Vic Brown, public relationist, makes a brisk announcement. "Over at Brown & Brown we held a little contest. I explained that it's a fund-raising ball and we needed a catchy name and, to make a long story short, the winner is . . ." Brown pulls out his scratch pad: "The Contrillion. Get it?"

A mutter of approval.

"Excuse me, Madam Chairman, I wonder what my chances are of being selected for the Decoration Committee," asks Myra.

Penny Benedikt grimaces. She's saving the post for her swanky friends. For her two-and-three-maid acquaintances. For her chauffeured, mansioned, *bon vivant* pals. Myra slumps in her chair as Mrs. Benedikt skillfully tables the motion. Well, Rose is as good as a dozen of those overpaid domestics. And she'd rather converse with a strange taxi driver any day than with one of those loverboy chauffeurs.

A deadly lull settles across the room. A dwarf of a physician is discussing the advantages of Cleopatra Vaginal Jelly, as the swanks, one by one, tiptoe out on their inordinately expensive shoes. Well, not her. She'll stay if it takes all night. Because what could be more important than too many people? Except atomic war. But that comes tomorrow. Or was it yesterday?

She concentrates on the droning dwarf. The nerve of those bored swells walking out on what must be terribly crucial because the knob-headed physician is raising his voice. How can you leave at a time when millions of people —men and women, widows, bachelors, the diseased, the infirm—are about to be crowded off the planet?

The dwarf points to a graph. His voice deepens, his eyes grow watery. He's looking directly at her, at Myra Russell, the only one who cares. Maybe the good doctor is going to propose a simple, pleasant and inexpensive solution to the world's woes. Myra listens with all her heart.

❧

Examination of the bedroom mirror: the image of a gregarious but disenchanted widow, a weary but community-conscious mother, a leisured but impoverished Seniority Citizen.

She's got to diet, economize, pull in her belt. Maybe she'll buy an account book, account for her hours, black and red inkstains depicting the balance of her days. Maybe, who knows, she'll be able to resist the midnight truffle, threatening this very minute to ruin her complexion. Maybe she'll uncover a brand-new skin cream, a new husband, a new life. Which can, she knows it, be beautiful.

But not tonight. She's too exhausted: lectures, card games, meetings—her unbearable clubwoman's burden.

"How can you be cleaning at midnight!" exclaims Myra, tossing her gloves on the table. Rose sulks in the corner. Suppressed, the kind who never thinks of anything but mopping. Scrubbing cupboards, poor creature, so she won't have to think about men. Who are, after all, unavoidable.

Rose replies with a cranky stare. "I'm cleaning at midnight 'cause I went out this afternoon with a boyfriend." Myra raises an eyebrow. Rose and her imaginary dreamboats. "Believe me, Mrs. Russell, it don't pay to be honest. What do you get for it? Nothing but calluses and hate. I feel so miserable, I could kill myself."

The same old suicide threat. Because she needs sympathy. Who doesn't these days? "Sorry, Rose dear. I completely apologize."

Myra closes her door, kicks off her shoes and reaches for the pills. Better to block out the entire fiasco.

She remembers that CHEMBAN lecture: people committing suicide out of sheer indifference. The bottle slips to the floor, spilling the narcotic capsules across the rug. No, she mustn't be indifferent. What would her husband say? Ralph, with his consuming passion for order. But Ralphy is gone. Let the pills fall where they may.

The TV tube glows with lurid colors. A silent movie about death. Myra twists the dial. Hurry, before she's fascinated. Last week it was so grisly she didn't dare turn off the lights. And electricity costs money. And money is the fuel she's running low on. And she must speak to someone or she'll go out of her mind. She snaps off the television, and dials a telephone SOS.

"Debbie, I'm having a terrible night. The evening's so long I'm being crucified."

"You don't know how lucky you are," counsels Debbie. "With your husband it was no fuss, no bother. Sure, Alex is suffering. But he's suffering so slowly, it's killing *me*.

"Myra, don't you dare! You've got to have faith. If you tell Alex you sold those shares, he'll have another relapse. You can't imagine what the last emergency cost. Oh goodness, he's screaming for me. In agony. I've got to run. Why don't you try the midnight movie? A wonderful ghost story."

The television winks at her with its evil glass eye. Myra turns to the stock market page.

Rose, in the living room tunes to an obscure station. A jazz band, a sextet of demolition players, bent on wrecking sleep. She'd beg her to turn it off, but Rose needs an outlet, too. Everyone does. It's a universal impulse. Even when you're suppressed. Which is why Rose hangs those pictures of film stars on her bedroom wall. Right next to her saints. Well, to the blissfully ignorant, saints and sinners are just alike.

12 ¼—an all-time low! She should never have sold. She should have waited for tomorrow, which must, by the law of averages, be better. But how can you live on tomorrows? D&K—Railroad of the Future. Alex's immortal sermon about faith. The faith which drove Ralph to his pauper's grave. The faith which is driving her in, too, as if Ralph needs company, and the only company he'll accept is Myra Russell, ever-faithful widow.

Nothing doing. She's got to be constructive. Myra turns a new leaf. *Devices for Controlled Living.* They'll be asking for her summary. What can she say, that it's too dull? An exploding population, starvation, fear, famine, dull? Dutifully, she plods past page seven. Hunger pains. She must resist. Gradually, inexorably, she's being surrounded by temptations—sleeping pills, television talkfests, éclairs at midnight.

She glances at her naked wrist. First thing in the morning she'll steal out and buy herself a watch. Of course it will cost a pretty penny. But time is a necessity and there's nothing you can do about necessities except give in.

Which is exactly the case with her tranquilizers. She gazes at them mournfully. Just one, enough for a few hours' shuteye. She'll think of it as a seasick tablet, and try to forget they're as dangerous as pesticides, as dangerous as dyed grapefruits. Which reminds her of CHEMBAN's expensive raffle drive.

Naturally she will. She'll have to as a good example. She'll give and she'll give generously. From the bottom of her heart. Which, let's face it, feels like an overwound clock. Must be her feverish imagination.

Myra reopens the financial page with its tales of woe and exultation. She examines the booming steels, healthy autos, skipping sick rails, continuing her journey among electronics, steady chemicals, soaring missiles. Who knows, her weary eyes flickering with exhaustion, maybe someday she'll discover a winner.

❧

A tip-top morning. A spectacular seminar. Rare diseases. Every moment diverting, every fact noteworthy. A divine two hours and thirty minutes according to the pendulum clock which hung, like a Damocles sword, above the passionate speaker. And now, amidst the splendor of the czars, she sits with her friend, Debbie Hilliard, in a choice and cozy corner of the Muscovite Tea House.

The plumed waitress stares haughtily as Myra glares at the luscious menu. All those necessary expenses, life, shelter and nutrition, an unholy trinity of absolute musts. What is she to do, turn herself into a living corpse! "Make that the de luxe economy," she commands. "With a squirt of vanilla on the Minsk pie."

"I'll just have the plain economy."

"On a diet?" inquires Myra, when the waitress is out of earshot.

"Economizing," mutters Debbie.

"I thought Alex was doing well."

"Medically, but not financially. Those round-the-clock nurses are so costly. Anyhow . . ." she confesses, "I'm afraid of the future."

"Now, now," shrugs Mrs. Russell like a confirmed optimist. "Don't you worry. Who knows, maybe Alex will be cured."

"That's not the problem," snaps Debbie. A moment of silence while the de luxe is gently spread before a starving Myra, while the unadorned economy is shoved before a sad-eyed Debbie. "Naturally you accept the inevitable. Becoming a widow is bound to happen. Like change of life. And I rather expect it's not really all that bad. Do as you please. *Laissez-faire*." A libertine glow emanates from Debbie's mascaraed eyes.

That's what you get for being repressed, a loose imagination. As if someday she intends to dis-repress herself! Well it's not easy when you're sixty plus like Debbie and refuse pharmaceutical therapy because you're stingy. Myra looks contemptuously at her friend anticipating widowhood like a bride who can't wait to be ravished.

"Sleep when you want," Debbie continues, "movies when you want, nightclubs. Right now, it's pure slavery. Myra, I have to watch those gorgeous nurses like a nighthawk. Alex gives me the shivers every time he smiles. This is his last chance and he knows it. What if one of them tricked him into falling in love?"

"Unbelievable," says Myra, dipping into her Odessa lobster on peasant rye. How does Debbie manage to keep so thin? By worrying about money, that's how. Well, she has never worried about bank accounts and she's not going to start now.

"If Alex changed his will, if one of those nurses convinced him he's still capable, I'd be left penniless, an impoverished widow."

Myra stops her munching. "An impoverished widow. That really would be awful." She examines her overloaded platter. She should never have ordered such a delightful luncheon. Far too expensive. As if she's eating a piece of her own estate, nibbling on the Danbury & Kent, the railroad to transport her through those golden, now tinsel years.

"I try my best," says Debbie, gobbling her cream cheese and Beluga jelly on toast. "I've chosen the homeliest nurses I can find. But Alex manages to get rid of them. I think he bribes them not to come back. And somehow the replacement is always pretty as a picture." She stares wistfully at a commanding ikon. "I have to stand guard day and night. The only reason I'm free right now is because fortunately the afternoon nurse is a beast." Debbie chuckles maliciously. "An absolute beast."

"Are you sure the beast is coming back?"

"What do you mean!" Debbie scowls at the unappetizing ladyfingers, as if they belong to an evil tart, painted fingernails and all.

"Suppose the beast has been replaced?"

"But she was just hired," cries Debbie, the suggestion beginning to take hold. "Myra, look how late it is. Never a dull moment. I've got to get going."

Mrs. Russell bites into Debbie's leftover Caucasian pickle. Neurotic personality. All she can think of is death and sex.

A ghoulish combination. Suddenly she remembers the unpaid bill. "Debbie! Debbie Hilliard! You forgot the . . ."

It does not pay to do business with a repressed half-widow, who will leave you high and dry the moment the right man appears. Better to be suppressed like Rose, or frustrated like Sybil. But what does it matter—suppressed, repressed, or even depressed?

Plenty. To be repressed like Debbie is to want to, but you freeze every time you think of it. To be suppressed like Rose means you never dare think of it. And to be frustrated like her daughter-in-law, means no matter how often you think of it, you can never be satisfied.

So where does that leave her? With the check, that's where. Yes, the wages of sex are sin, and the wages of generosity are unpaid bills. Myra fishes for her handbag. It won't budge an inch. Feigning illness. For the sake of her estate, her future, her twenty more years of widowhood, the clasp on her most expensive pocketbook absolutely refuses to open.

The plumed waitress waits grimly for her de luxe tip.

❧

Alone in New York, surrounded by strangers, she could fall dead this very moment and no one would notice. She could drop to the gutter, moaning with agony, her skull fractured, her brain deranged, her arms and legs mangled like an Irish stew. And they'd just step over her, staring at the pitiful mess as if it were nothing but a picturesque problem for the sanitation department.

Maybe she'll move. A small town where folks would care. They'd nod to her in the streets: "Howdy, Mrs. Russell, fine day, isn't it?" "That's the Widow Russell, poor thing. My, doesn't she look good." "Afternoon, Mrs. Russell, you certainly seem chipper." A friendly, homey town where every happening is cause for concern, where everyone's concern is a cheerful cause.

Nonsense, she'd be bored stiff! Why, it would be nothing but one continuous lull. She's in New York and she's got to make the best of it. Because life is too full of perilous todays to think about tomorrows. She must forget these pastoral fantasies and hurry, hurry, the museum is about to close.

Myra pauses at the booth marked *Education*. A hasty choice of lectures: Greek, Indic, Erotic, Messianic. She changes her mind to Cretan. That disposes of Mondays perfectly. From two till four. Time enough for a hurried snack at Schrafft's, time to scamper to the museum, just in time to pull out her notebook, don her thinking cap and start delving into the art of Crete. Yes, a new world has begun to unfold. Maybe she'll become a sort of expert. Only that would take years. And time, let's face it, is something she has got to ration.

Cretan Art it is. An auspicious beginning. She adds her florid signature to the gilded register, noting the other addresses. Exactly the element she likes to associate with. She must crib a copy when no one's looking. For CONTROL's high-class mailing.

Five, six, seven for Cretan I. Egyptology has twelve. But that's on Friday, her CHEMBAN night. She'll simply have to do with Cretan.

"Tuition fee!" her shock hidden behind a smile. "I thought it was free. A public service. Why, I never realized . . ." The line behind her mutters impatiently. Spidery black widows, staring with their restless jet eyes. "Of course," she concedes. "I must have misread the brochure," as her pen scribbles out an illegible check.

A financial strain. But what is she to do, squander a whole blue Monday fretting in her apartment like a mummy, wondering where in the world her dynastic treasure could be? For a single miserable check, her Monday afternoons are now guaranteed to be fascinating. And educational, as well.

And expensive, as well. Of course she could dispose of Rose. Rose, with nobody to turn to, with no place to go. Like herself. Except now she *will* have a place to go. To the Museum of Fine & Distinguished Art.

She should, she knows it, economize, moving from six spacious rooms to a single cubicle, letting Rose sleep behind a Chinese lacquer screen. But the antique screen would cost a fortune. And so would a convertible Swedish couch. And she can no more rid herself of old furniture than she can undo her former life. She strolls past the Egyptian statues, their granite hands outstretched like beggars.

Perhaps she could fill her Monday afternoons in the library, searching for a good book. At least Monday evenings are occupied. And with odd Thursdays, even Tuesdays, Wednesday noons and Sunday mornings, the week will pass over her like a delightful whirlwind. She certainly is a bustling individual when you compare her to Debbie, hopelessly waiting for Alex to stage his demise.

Myra meditates. Her dwindling estate, an approaching sixth decade, an indifferent son, the city itself, now immersed in smog, buried in garbage, crawling with thieves, pickpockets, rapists. She pictures the koolie birds in the heart of liberated Africa, the last of their kind, about to be snared, speared, about to be sent into extinction. Which is exactly where she's heading if she doesn't do something positive.

"A refund if you don't mind," murmurs Myra, anxiously eyeing the cash register. "You see, I forgot. I mean about Cretan I. I'm awfully sorry, but Mondays are completely absorbed." Grabbing her check, she rushes toward the exit, past sphinxes and hieroglyphic warnings, past Byzantine fetishes and medieval flagellations, into the gaudy, intoxicating air of her beloved East Side with its millions of urgent diversions.

How in the world does Rose occupy her afternoons? She doesn't shop, rarely chats about movies, never about art, scarcely mentions friends, has no relatives, is scared of men, possesses no interests, is interested in no possessions.

After twenty years, her domestic is a complete mystery. Who knows if she's really a widow? Probably a wild story. That's what you get for making yourself unwanted: an imaginary lover and a suppressed sex drive.

It's not just suppression that's Rose's downfall, it's having so little to do: vacuum cleaners do her rugs, scrubwomen do her floors, laundromats do her linens.

But this is New York, not a busybody village. And what

occupies her maid is her maid's affair. Still, just to have something to think of, Myra can't help wonder.

Maid's day off. That means no dinner. Being dependent on a domestic for all these years was utter folly. Soon she'll be sixty, a time to be finally happy. And just look at her, her lips all smeared, her heart pounding like a sledge hammer, her trembling fingers, that nervous tic on her lower chin, her eyelash half off, her platinum wig down to her nose . . .

"Debbie, this is Myra. I'm having a sluggish afternoon. Thought I'd call and say hello. No, I'm sticking with the railroad rain or shine." How do the Hilliards think she survives, on Ralph's miserable insurance? That was spent ages ago. "Tell Alex to take care. Health is a necessity. Dinner? I'm always calling at the wrong time. What are you going to have?" A delicious inventory. Myra's salivary glands discharge with envy.

"You know how it is when Rose is off. It means some luncheonette. And SANITY isn't till nine. Debbie, I realize how frantic you are, being a martyr to Alex. But I do wish you'd stop for a while and join up. There is such a thing as community feeling. I mean if there's a war, we'll all be goners, without exception. Oh, the nurse. Of course you have to be careful. I only wish Ralph had been. I mean his investments. I'm not blaming Alex one iota. The railroads will see good days again, I'm sure. Only I wish they'd hurry. Debbie, I've got to run. Yes, Paul. They've invited me. He and Sybil are up to their necks in work. Scarcely breath enough to say hello."

She'll drop in casually. After all, he's her son. Not that she interferes. But a mother has certain obligations and that includes the obligation to drop in. Even without notice. Even for dinner.

Grabbing her handbag, she dashes to the elevator, wondering how Rose can fill an entire afternoon with no one to talk to, with nothing but time on her hands. Well, some people are just plain eccentric.

❧

"Crooks, all of 'em," shouts the cab driver, hurtling down the slippery avenue. "Every mayor, councilman, judge. Why else would they want the job? Power! And when I say power, I mean dough, mazuma, the green stuff."

"Indeed," says Myra. An incredibly intelligent man. Too bad. A round peg in a squared-off hole.

"Y'read about the Super-Bomb? Why should the government build one that big? The owners of them California war factories pay a kickback, that's why."

Wonderful how SANITY has reached the man in the street. Probably a paid-up member. Then where's his sword-and-plowshare button? Afraid of offending a conservative customer, no doubt.

"I been in two wars and I can tell you the whole thing's a racket. The army's a racket, the government's a racket, even Wall Street's a racket."

"You can say that again," she notes bitterly.

"Defense is a racket, these giveaway programs are a racket, this welfare business is a racket. Hell, even Civil Rights is getting to be a racket."

An agnostic. But an earnest one, an outspoken one. And

28

that's what counts, to speak out. "I'm against war, too," she affirms. "I mean the damage it does is ridiculous. Think of the waste of resources, talent, energy. Not to mention time."

"You said it, lady. It's all one helluva racket," as they scatter a crowd of jaywalkers.

"Greenwich Village," she directs. "My son's place. He's invited me for dinner. I know how confusing it is for taxis. They say the avenues follow the original cowpaths, that's why they're so crooked."

"Everything's crooked."

"Yes, the houses, the streets, even the names are old-fashioned. That's why Paul lives there. Because he and his wife like things the way they were."

"Can't beat the old days."

"Quite right, Mr. . . . Reilly," reading the hack license.

Myra smiles gracefully. It's as if she's met a new friend. Why not? He *is* a friend. So are those jaywalkers down the street. Everyone. Just lend a hand, extend a smile and whisper a kind word. Eight million New Yorkers mean eight million potential friends.

The limousine scoots down the cobbled lanes. "Boy," the cabbie is saying, "they certainly don't build things like that nowadays. Today it's all tarpaper and plasterboard. Phoney, that's what. Those new apartments won't even last our lifetime. Phoney lumber, phoney workmanship, phoney addresses for phoney people. The whole world's heading down a drainpipe. And even the drainpipe's phoney."

"I couldn't agree more," says Myra. "That's why we've got to continue the fight for . . ." Before she can begin her speech, the taxi screeches to a halt.

29

She'd like to explain that there *are* things a person can do. But it wouldn't seem right lecturing while the meter relentlessly ticks away. As if she's paying to be heard.

She gives her recently-discovered friend a much-too-generous tip.

"Hey, thanks."

"Not at all, Mr. Reilly," beams Myra as the cab door snaps in her face. "It was my pleasure." Pleasure. Treasure. She could use a brain like his, helping her to unravel the clue, the map, the . . .

Before she can finish, the taxi rushes off. Her fellow treasure hunter is gone forever.

Greenwich Village: tattooed sailors and Black Muslim criers, Gray Line gawkers and doorway deviants, gold-hearted hustlers and psychedelic daydreamers—a wonderful place to keep occupied.

A curlicued sign: B. Halpern—Caricaturist. "Only a couple of bucks," says the artist, adjusting his beret. "Two minutes for your authentic portrait."

"No rush," replies Myra, settling into a three-legged stool. "I've all the time in the world." She poses with a smile. Which is so hard to maintain these days. Especially a genuine smile. And the portrait must be genuine, not mere pastel flattery. "Try to catch the color of my hair," as the artist looks her over. "It's not really grayish, you know. If you examine it, you'll see loads of other shades. I don't believe in touching up. A person should be what she is. Besides, those hair dyes contain chemicals. That's how people get follicle fallout and cancer of the scalp. Because women are so vain, they'd rather kill themselves and look beautiful, than be horrible and look alive."

She tries to catch a forbidden glimpse of her half-formed face. The artist cleverly shields the portrait from her prying eyes. Temperamental. Still, it's an excellent way to spend one's waking hours. Always concentrating. How shall I draw the lips? Has she a sour face or a pleasant one? Pleasant, of course. That is, considering her mature circumstances. Myra smiles. The painter rises haughtily. Two dollars plus a gracious tip emerge from her weary purse. No, it wouldn't be right to peek. Not in front of the original artist. It might discourage him. People like that want nothing but praise. Who doesn't?

Ghastly! The hair is gray as granite, the eyes as grim as death. Couldn't he at least have made the wrinkles natural? Of course she has lines, but not that many and not that deep. She looks a hundred times more refined. Maybe even more beautiful. Every artist takes liberties, true. But liberty doesn't mean license. Not when you demand two dollars from a sitter whose only goal is honesty and a little compassion.

She wanders along the cobbled mews marked *Residents Only*. Filled with thousands of tourists' faces: freckled, old, haggard, brown, yellow—there's nothing like variety.

Her jeweled fingers rap against the tiny Federal door. An intimate miniature. That's why they don't have children. Accommodations for only two. Anyhow, why bring babies into a world that's so disturbed?

31

"What a surprise!" snaps Sybil.

"Just enjoying the sights," smiles Myra. "Thought I'd drop in and say hello."

"Paul's up to his neck in work, but . . ." Myra forces her way in.

"What Paul needs is leisure. Same as me. Though I wouldn't object to a career." Foolish remark. As if she could start a career at fifty-nine about to touch sixty.

Myra gazes past the antique beams as Paul gesticulates angrily. "Got to," he shouts. "The only tract left. Parks, hell. What Happiness Homes needs is space," she overhears. "There'll always be plenty of customers. It's land that's scarce, not people."

"Paul can't see you tonight," confides Sybil. "You should have phoned."

As if she needs permission to see her own son! "Hello," Myra cries.

Paul looks up from his early-American rocker. "Hi, Mom. Sorry I don't have time. Business."

"Don't work too hard," she cautions, throwing a kiss past the converted kerosene lantern.

A six-foot-six gentleman sits at the edge of the Quaker couch. It's D'Agostino, the one who addressed them at the meeting. Myra nods. He doesn't even remember. That's the trouble with CONSERVE, too impersonal.

Sybil whisks her into the breakfast nook. Pine-knotted walls lined with honest faces, primitives by original painters. Like the one who just sketched her. But these, at least, are truthful. That's the way it was in those days. Honesty was the best policy.

"Myra, I wish we could invite you for dinner, only . . ." Sybil's teeth are clenched.

"I wouldn't dream of it. I mean, I hate to be a nuisance. But SANITY is just around the corner, and it's Rose's day off, so I decided to kill some time. Sightseeing. If only I had a place like this. What a fascinating way to keep busy. I mean the restoration. Must be costing you a fortune cookie."

Sybil looks dour. "A pity you can't come and live with us." An embarrassed pause. "Only these stables are strictly for two."

"I wouldn't dream of it. Rose and I are perfectly happy where we are. Naturally I wish it weren't so expensive, but . . ."

"That's what I've been wanting to talk to you about, Mother."

Mother. What a strange expression. Myra tries to hide her suspicions.

"I know how Paul always jokes about Maisonettes specializing in widows and fairies. But it's an up-and-coming field. After all, homosexuals have to live somewhere, too."

"Indeed," says Myra, refusing to be reactionary.

"And I don't have to tell you," Sybil lowers her voice, "how husbands are dying off faster than wives. That leaves a surplus of widows. People like you, too active to care for a large establishment."

She looks into Sybil's caprine eyes. Sublimation. Making up for her sterility. If you can't have children, why wear your husband to the bone for a hopeless whim? Better to be like Rose and never think about it, or to be a Debbie, constantly fighting it.

33

"Mother, it's a crime the way you keep selling those stocks just to keep up with the Joneses."

"I see," shrugs Myra. The odor of old-fashioned apple dumplings. She'd like to step into the kitchen and help out. But it wouldn't be right. Anyhow, she doesn't know a thing about stoves. Anyhow, she was just passing by. Just to say hello.

"Hello and g'bye," cries Myra. "Got to get a move on. Besides having a meeting, I've an awful problem. A crossword puzzler. What rhymes with blue?" *Adieu!* The treasure is *adieu.* Meaning farewell treasure. Meaning . . .

"Paul thinks it's wonderful the way you keep occupied without having anything to do. I mean without a job."

"Keeping occupied," says Myra, looking at D'Agostino, whose *no, no's* reverberate throughout the dwarf-size house, "keeping occupied is the most important problem in life."

Paul nods. D'Agostino scowls. Sybil begs her to think it over. "Maisonettes. Just right for you, Mother. Luxurious living for active, thrifty people."

Myra waves good-bye, then races across the cobblestone alley. She's got to hurry and grab a thrifty snack. Anyhow, she can't stand Sybil's antiquated cooking. Not that she can remember. It's been so long. But who knows, maybe someday they'll invite her again.

Meanwhile, she'll eat alone and lump it.

Down the quaint streets. A kaffee-klatsch of poker-faced housewives, sipping muddy espressos. Befuddled bachelors, licking frozen custards, wondering what comes next. Ecstatic LSD'sters. Delicious homemade pizzas. Handwrought jewelry: brass-knuckle wedding rings, jinxed amulets, intriguing crucifixes. A resplendent Buddha, an exquisite candlestick from Scotland, an expressive painter from Brooklyn. An explosion of tourists, jamming every shoppe, packing every cranny, filling the historical lanes with hysterical laughter.

She steps into The Adult Learning Foundation with its zany spiral architecture. "Your catalogue," she asks the tweedsy woman at the desk. A Lesbian, no doubt. Takes all kinds. Not that she's to blame. Why, that tweedsy woman could have been a widow like herself. Possibly she found her days just one lull after another. Fell into a sordid trap. No escape. A life of sin. Maybe—who knows—it could happen to her!

Myra sits in a best-design chrome-and-leather settee. The pigskin squeals painfully, straining to uphold her. With each motion of her sturdy frame, she can hear the grunt. She must launch into that new miracle diet. Tomorrow morning, first thing after breakfast. Maybe she'll become trim again, attractive again. It's either that or . . . She stares at the tweedsy woman. The woman stares back, then smiles lasciviously. Myra buries her blue-gray head in the catalogue.

Each course is so delightful, she scarcely knows which to choose. *The Meaning of Human Existence–Part III.* But she hasn't mastered II yet. *Esthetics for the Connoisseur.* Excellent, only she's no connoisseur. And never will be, not on her budget. *Love and the Global Crisis.* Just what the doctor ordered. Wednesdays 6-8. Perfect. A perfect insertion for her six-to-eight, midweek lulls. With barely enough time to dash to her 8:30 CONSERVE. Myra casually inquires the price.

She drifts away, straining to shield her tears. Far too expensive. Ralph, oh Ralphy, why weren't you more cautious? Alex didn't mean to put *all* your money into that miserable, dilapidated D&K.

Maybe it *wasn't* all the money. What about that mysterious cache, buried behind a light switch, concealed beneath a Persian carpet. Ralph's last words, his shaky command, his muttered bequest: *"I treasure . . ."* Then a blank, death snatching the clue from her outstretched hand. And Ralph, staring at the bookcase with its best sellers. Myra shouting: "What treasure? Tell me!" His vacant eyes gazing at her as if, having interred his fortune like some piratical tyrant, he'd been stabbed in the back.

But of course! A treasure map. Hidden in one of those unread condensations. Tomorrow, first thing after she starts her diet, she'll dust off the secret volume, unfold the map, pace off the distances and uncover it: a trunk loaded with fervent IOU's, with slightly chipped diamonds, with gold-backed promissories. Myra Russell, the well-to-do widow. She'll be able to afford *Love and the Global Crisis. Human Existence III*, as well. Private tutors, fabulous bridge lessons, lush cocktail lounges. Meetings, too. Just because she's rich doesn't mean she lacks conscience. She must never forget the world is in a mess and she's part of it. But somehow, with the treasure, Ralph's rainy-day treasure, tucked safely away in her imaginary handbag, Myra finds it hard to believe.

❧

Mrs. Russell sits alone in the Adobe Hacienda determined to look hopeful. A Negress, sombrero on head, hands her the Castilian menu. Myra examines the drawing, a sickly-green cactus with venomous spines. "Wouldn't you care to make a suggestion?" she says, trying to be helpful.

"Number two's O.K. Number four combination's better."

"What's a tortilla?" as she rapidly calculates the bill. Suppose she finds the magic volume and the treasure map is gone? What if Rose, by some dreadful accident, threw it out? No, this is an adventure in good eating and she must make the best of it.

"Tortilla," explains the Negress, "corn dough baked on tin. Never had it but once. Made me sick."

"Well, I certainly want to avoid that kind of delicacy." She wanders into the more expensive section at the bottom. A la carte. But you only live once. Which reminds her. SANITY. A talk on extermination. She has got to get a move on. "*Mole*, what's that?"

"Hot," warns the waitress. "Burns your insides out. If you're scared, they make it cool."

"Which way do the natives like it?" asks Myra. "That's the way I want it."

"I'm not a Mexican, lady. How would I know?"

"Oh, but I thought you were. I mean, with that strange costume and those beads, I thought you were a visitor, perhaps. Working her way around the world." She glances at the menu. "I thought you might be doing this to pay for your travels. So you could visit different countries. Europe, Canada, Africa . . ."

The waitress's eyes examine her coolly. The cook, who she thought for sure was genuine Mexican, has stepped out of the kitchen. A Chinaman!

"*Mole*," cries Myra. "Make it," shouting to the beady-eyed cook, "hot! I want the real thing."

Everyone in the intimate restaurant is gobbling, complaining. Couples breaking up, lifetime friendships being severed, everyone perturbed but her.

Myra sits there, hypnotized by her jewel-free, economy, wind-it-yourself watch. Two hours to go. A deathly lull hovers over her table. The cuisinary adventure no longer seems so venturesome. She opens *The Adult Learning* catalogue. She'll have to investigate the curriculum thoroughly, glancing at the descriptions, picturing the learned professors, envisioning her brain's improvement.

One hundred and five more minutes to go. Oh, how she'd like to stab them, strangle them, till the hours are dead and she's eaten the lonely *mole* and time, like the red-hot dinner, has vanished into her digestive system. Thank goodness for the cream puff and the catalogue and her interesting schedule or the hours would be years.

Hurry! Her economy watch is five minutes slow. Not a minute to waste! She shoves the cold remains of her uneatable Mayan *mole* down her throat, thrusts out a generous tip, and, half choking, rushes headlong toward the Avenue of America.

From an intriguing dinner to a fascinating meeting. The evening grows more delightful every second. Like an old-fashioned revival hour, full of fun and fury, signifying a lot and costing but a little.

"Peace," shouts Vic Brown, "is old hat. A thousand other organizations are demanding the same thing. Let's stand out a bit."

Myra agrees. Follow Victor and you're never behind the times.

"Since when is peace a dirty word?" demands Sid Tannenbaum. "Since when are we, the humble members of SANITY, too proud to beg for peace, too sophisticated to demand a truce? Ask the men who died at Verdun if peace is old hat. Ask . . ."

Verdun, is that north or south of Paris? If only she had an atlas.

". . . ask those corpses in Korea, those burning bodies in Saigon, those mutilated infants of Hiroshima . . ."

Myra feels sick. Must be that *mole*.

"Peace in our time is out of style," insists SANITY's public relationist. "Strictly for appeasers. We need a new word, not so militant. Something unique, encompassing and catchy. Or else SANITY will become just another cog in a flat tire."

A brilliant man. How can you compare Vic Brown who deals with ideas all day long, to Sid Tannenbaum, a jewelry designer for idle women. A divorcé. Though possibly it is more rational to live on a miserable alimony than to stick it out with someone who, for better or worse, you absolutely can't stand. But attention must be paid. A vital debate: war and peace, life and death. Before you know it,

39

another contentious Monday will have vanished into history.

She's spoken too soon. They debate the motion to table peace. A legalistic lull. Well, if time were always interesting, nothing would ever get done.

First Myra sides with Vic and the Beggars. Demand too much from life and you'll end up empty handed. The Beggars are quite right.

Then she turns to the left and Tannenbaum's Bombastics. If you don't speak out, you'll never be heard. Look at Ralph, too shy to ask about the railroad. Did it have any passengers? Did it even have locomotives? Afraid to question, to doubt, to insist.

Then she re-aligns with Victor. SANITY must create a pleasant image. Does she go outside with her hair uncombed, her cheeks unrouged, her dress unpressed? Vic's faithful promise: a million extra signatures if they'll only change the wording from *demand* to *request*.

Why not? What's in a verb? For a million signatures a small compromise won't hurt anyone.

"Never!" cries Tannenbaum. "It's a crime against our charter, against the millions of soldiers who died in Korea, against the mothers who perished in Nagasaki, against the . . ."

Myra knows she ought to agree. Although it's no crime to be intolerant just because he's Jewish. How depressing to belong to a minority group. Which is probably why he's fixated on peace.

Brown proposes a drive to rent billboards, spread the

word; love and tranquillity plastered across America. Contrary to every principle of CONSERVE, her nature group.

But isn't it more important to conserve peace than to save a few yards of scenery, a tree here and there? Anyhow, they can build the billboards between the trees. That way no one will get hurt.

"I've got a motto that's a beaut," continues Vic. "It's hopeful, optimistic, realistic and . . ." looking at Tannenbaum, "it gets our image across. Ready?"

Myra holds her breath.

"PEACE IS PRECIOUS!"

Another prolonged debate. Another prolonged lull. That's the trouble with democracy, too many lulls.

The motion is tabled. The billboards, too. Now, thank goodness, she won't have to boost one cause by betraying another. She wonders what opera she'll have to sit through next Thursday. But is it an odd Thursday? She consults her mental calendar. Movie at 4, dinner at 6, nothing at 8. An even Thursday, vacant, like one of Paul's wretched Happiness Homes, just waiting for someone to move in.

Why is she daydreaming when they're discussing the most important problem in the world, her problem, too—survival!

The Cinema Committee Report. Tannenbaum begins his oration. "The peace films I've screened are rubbish, doodles, contrived nonsense. All but one, a film in progress. No, it's not being made by some advertising hack . . ." Victor looks gloomy. ". . . trying to save his soul through social protest. And it's not an arty improvisation, either. No, ladies

41

and gentlemen, this film is being shot by a ten-year-old boy. That's right, an innocent ten-year-old who's shooting the entire project behind his parents' back.

"No, he's not using fake actors with fake makeup and fake smiles. No phoney sets, phoney lights, or phoney costumes. He's filming this with real, natural people in everyday streetclothes on ordinary streetcorners, in God-given, natural sunlight. No, he's not using some clumsy thirty-five millimeter camera on an expensive dolly. He's not even using a sixteen millimeter with a tripod. This pure boy, this mere child, this kid genius, is using the film of the people. An everyday Kodak with everyday eight millimeter black and white!"

How touching. If only she were his mother. They could be a team, making movie after movie about peace, war, love. If only she had a son who really loved her.

"This untutored, uninhibited lad is creating a picture to be called *The Horrors of Hate*. Some will say it's immoral. Some will say it's degenerate, disgusting, pornographic. But I say it's great. And I say it's the film SANITY's Cinema Committee has been looking for. The movie to move men's minds. Up to now, he's been making this picture with his own meager allowance. But the boy's in debt, out of film and frankly discouraged. Which is why I ask you, you who would lay down your lives for peace, to reach into your souls and enable this lad to go on with his cause."

Sensing a collection, the members fold up their tents and noisily steal away. But not her. Not for all the treasure in Arabia. A beautiful tale. As Tannenbaum passes by with his converted army helmet, Myra's handbag opens automatically.

"Hi, Mrs. Russell."

"Hello, Sid dear," she smiles shyly. "That was a splendid presentation. I took in every word. So fascinating, I can scarcely believe the evening's over."

She fishes for a bill. *Disgusting, Degenerate, Pornographic.* Never mind, the child must finish, nothing must deter. "Here's ten." Myra drops it like a discarded candy wrapper into the bullet-pocked helmet. "*The Horrors of Hate.* I'm sure it'll be a hit."

She stares into her despairing purse with its dozens of membership cards, some expired, some overdue, a few paid up. She'll have to cash more shares. "Could you, Mr. Tannenbaum, loan me a dollar back? I meant to donate nine," she whispers. But Sid is vanished, the members have all gone, the gloomy room with its poster pleas for SANITY lies abandoned.

En route home, Myra decides on another hurried visit. Just one more quick hello, a friendly nod. She stares up at the tiny window. Lights out. Except for the kerosene lantern in the bedroom. Shadows flickering across the calico curtain. Paul's, then Sybil's.

She studies her watch. It's too late. It wouldn't be polite, right in the middle of . . . Naturally her daughter-in-law means well. When you're as sterile as Sybil, you've got to keep trying.

It's poor Paul who has to pay the consequences. That's what happens when you marry against your parents' advice.

43

That mustache of Sybil's is growing bushier every day. Something wrong with the hormonal balance. A goat, that's what she's beginning to look like. So much sex drive, she's turning into a man. Which is what happens when you're frustrated and can never have enough. You get to be like Ralph, making a hobby out of it. As if sex is a reasonable way to occupy one's time. Which possibly it is for men. But not for women; they're not built for it.

Neither is Paul, up there in his Colonial four-poster, trying his best to appease Sybil, to keep her entertained.

If you can't have a child, you can't. Be satisfied. One less child means one less hungry mouth to feed. Her own mouth is starting to water. She must rush to the refrigerator and grab a quick bite before her morning diet begins.

Maybe, while quietly munching, she'll solve the riddle of the missing treasure. That's just when it's most likely to come to her, when she's in a total depression, when she's not even thinking. Myra Russell, her mind a void, stares up at the bedroom window. "Just stopped by on my way," she'd like to cry out. "Can't stay but a minute."

Why bother? They're obviously too involved, too frenzied, too fascinated to spare her a simple, courteous hello.

❧

Russell vs. Hilliard, a troubled conversation: "You're lucky you can fritter away so much leisure. For me, it's Alex and his nurses, morning, noon and midnight."

"Having leisure isn't so easy. Not when you're a widow without an ounce of security."

"Myra, don't you dare sell out! That's his final advice.

When highways get too crowded, they'll flock back to the railroads like homing pigeons. Alex says it'll be a true renaissance. He says you've got to have faith."

"Yes, faith, the biggest problem of all."

The taxi grinds to a halt. A Sunday tie-up. Automotive curses, threats, groans. Myra and Debbie stare through the carbon monoxide cloud at the strangulated traffic. Time for a momentary reflection.

If she had a drop of sense, she'd rid herself of Rose. Twenty years of widowhood. That's ten times the sentence she's served. How Rose takes her mind off her suppressions, only an analyst would know. Daydreams, probably. Not that Rose realizes what she's missing. She's barely intelligent enough. That's the trouble with education, it makes you too dissatisfied. Which is why it wasn't so bad she skipped Vassar and was forced to marry Ralph.

Only with Alex in the stock game, Debbie won't end up an everyday widow. She'll be a rich one. Just give the word and an entertaining evening will be hers. A snap of bored fingers and *voilà*, a fascinating new language, Brazilian, Castilian. Caught in an inescapable lull? Just count out the bills and open sesame, get whisked away on a magic-carpet tour. Yes, if you must be a widow, there's only one kind to be—a rich one.

"Oh dear!"

"What's the trouble?" asks Myra, snapping out of her séance.

"I forgot my purse," Debbie groans.

"Let me . . ." Myra is about to say *lend*. How stingy can you be? Especially on Sunday when you're going to church. Not that it's just a church. It's much better; it's a whole philosophic system. "Let me pay," announces Myra, examining the contents of her gutted handbag. Alex or no Alex, faith or no faith, she'll sell a few shares first thing tomorrow morning. Which will mean a scintillating trip to her broker, then a siesta at Schrafft's, a shopping binge on Fifth Avenue, a frozen dinner with Rose, a hurried hello to Paul, an urgent meeting of SANITY, a last-minute midnight snack, and her day, thank goodness, will be done.

The Carnegie Hall entrance overflows with women, stout and shriveled, agitated and serene. Widows in search of solace. No, information; solace, as they say at Divine Technology, is an anachronism. Myra hands the driver a bountiful tip. Poor wretch, think of having to work on a holiday. But at least it gives him something to do. Which, in the long run, is the most pressing problem in life.

Every seat is occupied. Like a sellout Broadway show. Only Broadway is shut tighter than a drum. And so are the department stores. Which is why it's fortunate the religions have agreed on Sunday, when there's nothing else to do. Not that Divine Technology is conformist. It's as much for the future as SANITY. Which is why she adores it. There's something uplifting about the future. And it certainly takes your mind off the present.

Myra examines the attractive swami. A splendid pear-shaped head. If only he doesn't have an accent.

"To Be or Not to Be? That is the dilemma of our times." Perfect English! In fact, too perfect. Oxford somewhere. She'll simply have to sit up and concentrate.

"He's rather handsome, don't you . . ."

46

"Shh!" warns Myra. She should never have brought a friend like Debbie. She should have invited someone intelligent. But who? Everyone she knows is either foolish or philosophically maladjusted. Which is no reason for gloom. After all, there are plenty of people she doesn't know. The problem is to find them. But meanwhile she's got to listen, and not just to her own distracting voice. No more sinking into a stupor like last week.

"Divine Technology means that progress is divinely ordained," explains the swami. "Which is why we must welcome it, no matter how bad it may seem." If it's not Oxford, it's probably Cambridge.

"We, of the DT faith, know that to oppose progress is is to oppose man's destiny. To oppose atomic research because of fallout is like opposing electricity because you might get a shock."

He's against SANITY! A conflict of causes. Like Happiness Homes, chopping the forest that CONSERVE is fighting to protect. Well, Happiness Homes isn't *her* cause, it's Paul's. And it's not a cause, it's a business. And anyhow, she had better concentrate or she won't be getting her ten dollars' worth.

"We, of the DT faith, must struggle to appreciate progress. For progress is Divine Will. This Divine and Omnipotent Will is expressed in our understanding of pathology, of necrology, of mob psychology, of rocketry, of each and every facet of nature's wisdom. Verily, I say unto you, to comprehend technology is to comprehend Him."

That magnetic swami makes her other groups look positively backward. As if they're desperately trying to halt progress. Which shouldn't be halted, not if there's nothing you can do about it. Suddenly she remembers. She's got to get a move on!

Hurry, she implores the speaker, now engaged in a complicated discussion about the electron microscope and how it's shattered our disillusionments. If only he'd glance at his chronometer.

"To conclude: God is a natural, inventive, progressive Force. To be aware of our Creator, is it not too much to ask ourselves—are we to be filled with understanding or are we not to be divinely inspired, forging ahead into an unknown, perhaps horrifying, perhaps happy future?"

"Well, what's the answer?" demands Debbie, as they shove their way out of the hall. "To be or not to be?"

"That's the question," explains Myra. "Divine Technology doesn't give answers, it gives you food for thought. Sometimes I can spend a whole evening mulling over what they've said. And even then I don't know. But it's obviously more advanced than the Presbyterians. Though I can't help wishing they'd break down and have an old-fashioned choir. The kind that makes chills run up your spine. Debbie, I've got to run like mad. Taxi, take me to the Atomic Energy Committee. Hurry, before it's too late!"

∾

I treasure . . . his incalculable last words. Did she mix up the syllables in her eagerness? *Why treasure?* As if Ralph, who lived only for money, in the last half-second of his life, had finally reformed.

Impossible! It's there. Rooted in that six-room labyrinth,

48

a luxuriant fiscal jungle, a tangle of green leaf banknotes. Myra, in her half-empty bed, wonders where.

If she were a husband and about to expire, where would she hide the cache? The last thing Ralph did before uttering the fatal clue was groan in agony, clutch his tummy, and curse her delicious grapefruit *pâté*.

Grapefruits. Are they berries or vegetables? Do you pick them or pluck them? Can you grow them in a hot house? In the throes of a lull, thank goodness for intellectual curiosity or she'd be absolutely bored to tears.

Myra wonders why art is so enriching, why sunsets are colorful, why husbands so dull. Why do stars twinkle, is there snow on Venus, are there people on Saturn? Myra wonders who invented—though she's certainly no atheist —God? How soon will the earth fill up with too many people, what will happen when there's no more coal, iron, salt, pepper? Why are more boys born than girls, why more widows than widowers, why more suicide in Sweden, where they're happy, than in New York, where—she can see it all around her—they're in despair. She should splurge for a change, buy herself a revised encyclopedia, one with answers to all the modern wonders and worries vexing her as she tosses in a midnight lull. An up-to-date, well-bound encyclopedia from the proceeds of a few D&K's. Which only yesterday plunged $3\frac{1}{4}$ points. She has got to sell more stocks and buy those cross-indexed answers to the thousand and one fascinating riddles which torture her sleep. Before the railroad, her aching heart, time itself reaches a final and irrevocable zero.

❧

Weekdays spell trouble: museums empty, streets abandoned, moviehouses deserted. Because they're drudging
away—sweatshops, sales counters, coal mines, anything to
keep busy. Well, she's too old to work and that is that.

But what would you call her labors for SANITY? As Sid
says, it's not the money that counts, it's the good you do.
Yes, she decides haughtily, she's just as hard a worker as
they are. Only a worker without salary, a worker whose
payment is peace, prosperity and pleasure. How bleak the
afternoon is beginning to seem.

Myra Russell, depressed daydreamer, turns her bloodshot
eyes toward the chess parlor. Filled with unoccupied seats
and forlorn tables. The wooden pieces, ready to do or die,
stare back at her, bewildered.

The wiry gentleman points to his neon sign: *The King's
Castle.* "It's a madhouse on weekends. More people than
seats. Weekdays, why stay open? Except, of course," he
points to the billboard, "my private tutoring." She glances
at the notice: *Igor Kovski INTERNATIONAL GRAND
MASTER. Austro-Hungarian Olympics. Lessons. Reasonable. Ask!*

"Could I come back when you're busy?" she asks. "I'd
love to learn something new. Card games are so tiresome. Besides, the women I know insist on playing for money.
Which is nothing but a drug. I used to play Mah-Jongg, but
that's old-fashioned. And so I have these empty Friday
afternoons and I noticed your little studio and I decided
chess might well be the answer to all my problems."

"The Game of Kings," notes Kovski, sipping his coffee.
Viennese. With whipped cream. She'll stay.

"Then I couldn't help reading your sign. Thirty cents an hour. Obviously less expensive than a movie. Anyhow, I've seen them all. The foreign ones, I mean."

"Sit. I'll demonstrate."

She pulls up a chair. The chair begins to sway. "I hope it's not difficult. I'm the kind with just so much patience. But once I discover something fascinating, I forget time completely."

"Chess," intones Kovski, setting up the wooden images, "is more complicated even than life."

"You don't say."

"Chess," dusting off the no-man's-land between the Negroes on his side and the whites which, Myra observes with pleasure, are hers, "the noble game of chess, for me it *is* life. Forty years. Every day, every night I work on the fantastic problems of these little armies."

Kovski illustrates the moves. "The object isn't," he explains, "annihilation. No, it's much more elegant. The goal in chess is to checkmate the king. Never mind the castles, those fortifications in the corners. Never mind the slaves, that army of pawns in the foreground. Never mind the horses, the bishops, the queen. It's the king that counts. Call him President, Prime Minister, Dictator. Trap him and you've won the election, the battle, the war."

This is the answer! She'll start practicing with Rose first thing in the morning. With Debbie in the afternoon. She'll carry her portable chessmen wherever she goes. In trains, taxis, everywhere, every moment her mind will be fully occupied. By *their* problems, not hers any more. She'll stay at home for good, hypnotized by her Game of Kings. No more outside diversions. She'll live within her income, hold on to her apartment, to Rose, to her board, that magic chessboard.

Her thoughts have wandered too far afield. "Would you please, Mr. Kovski, explain the moves again? You see, dear, I'm a slow beginner. But when I learn, I'm like an elephant." She squirms uncomfortably in the narrow chair. "Nothing can make me forget."

Kovski, his thin face twitching with impatience, reviews the possibilities. "The castle can only move in straight lines. The horses can only gallop, the pawns can only crawl."

So fearfully complicated, she can already feel her brain reeling. "A coffee break," she pleads, ordering it black to keep her stimulated. "If I have to concentrate one more minute, I think I'll come down with a headache. Guess I just don't have the mentality of a man."

"True," says Kovski, "a woman's never won the world championship. But there's a separate division for ladies, so don't be discouraged. The main thing is to start early."

"Two," says Myra, "o'clock."

"I started playing at five," says Kovski.

What an interesting person. She can't wait to tell Debbie Hilliard. But Debbie won't give a fig. She's all tied up with Alex and his legacy. "Five," she repeats. "An early age. I myself am," forcing a smile, ". . . forty-five."

Kovski examines her more closely.

"I always say you're never too late to learn," she adds.

The master looks noncommittal. An honest person. The only kind of teacher to have.

"In Europe," he blows across his coffee, trying to cool it.

Myra does the same. "In the old world, chess masters were treated like royalty. Noblemen invited us to their palaces as honored guests. Paid us royally, too. A whole chain of palaces, like you have motels in this country. The royal circuit, and we, the minstrels of the intellect. But in America, no intellect, no respect. Noblemen, extinct. Patrons, gone. Chess masters, finished. It's a new world."

Myra looks glum. "In my country they don't have enough time. You see, thinking means nothing to busybodies. That's why Americans don't worry about the Bomb. That's why I joined SANITY."

"SANITY, nonsense. They don't know how to use their minds," grumbles Kovski. "Listen, every problem is soluble, that's the cardinal rule in chess. But with SANITY, it's all trial and error, like a baby."

Myra moves her bishop to king's knight five. Igor snatches it with his pawn.

"The famous Serf Defense," Kovski explains. "Looks like a defense, only it's really a vicious attack."

"Well, it's better to take out frustrations in a game," she concedes, "than to do it in real life." Her castles crumble; her last pawn is sucked into Igor's black trap.

"I've got it figured out," says Kovski. How can he play and talk simultaneously? She tries to pay attention as her white queen encounters disaster. "What the world needs is a minor calamity. Like shock therapy. Catastrophic, but not permanent. For example," charging into Myra's dwindling battalion, "one summer a nuclear submarine should be sabotaged off Atlantic City. The ocean would be contaminated. People wouldn't be able to swim. Their vacations would be ruined. If they tried escaping to the mountain resorts, an atomic plane should mysteriously explode in the foothills. Let them stew for a summer in the sweltering cities and you'd see how they'd suddenly get interested in atomic disarmament. And if you want to stir up the Jews, just sabotage Miami Beach during their High Holy Days. Make the danger of atomic warfare hit home. Make Americans suddenly realize how the charming little world they take for granted is truly wretched. Checkmate!"

Myra shrugs with resignation. After all, you can't expect to beat a chessmaster on your first try. For thirty cents, what better way to spend one of her more expendable hours.

"That will be thirty dollars, Mrs. . . ."

"Russell," says Myra, reeling from the shock. "Only the sign says thirty cents."

"That's for players, Mrs. Russell. But a lesson from a Grand Master, head of the Austro- Hungarian Olympic . . ."

"Of course it's worth it," insists Myra, holding out the last of her tens. "Only you forgot to charge me for the coffee."

"Complimentary." Kovski dumps the dregs into the steaming percolator. "Yes, Mrs. Russell, a minor catastrophe. That's what this country needs to wake it from its slumber. A limited disaster which will immunize our planet from total annihilation."

"Fascinating," says Myra, snapping shut her pocketbook. "I mean that defense. Someday you must explain how it works. And the conversation is certainly worth pondering.

I've always said if we could put our best minds to work for peace as they work for war," she stares at her shattered white forces, "the world would be a better place to live in. Anyhow, I've got to run."

❧

Why should it be so hot in May? She'll have to buy that encyclopedia. Think how long it will take to travel from A to Z. Think of all the other things to do besides encyclopedias. Or is it encyclopediae? All those unexplored institutions: that Museum of Nature, the Museum of Science, that delightful one on Money. Think of all the exotic restaurants, the curiosity shops, of all the historic monuments still unvisited. Grant's Tomb, The Hall of Fame, the Statue of Liberty. Of course, that would be more interesting to immigrants like Tannenbaum and Rose O'Connor, who aren't so . . .

"Dr. Ackerman is waiting," whispers the sanitized nurse.

Myra glances at her watch. How thrilling to be a physician. Night calls, emergencies, a whole lifetime passing into glorious oblivion. Paul should have studied medicine. But he's made his bed with Sybil, so let them lie in it. For her, it was enough to be a plain everyday housewife. Only now she doesn't even have a house. Like a nun without a cloister. She stares at the nurse's spotless habit. That's what she should have been, a doctor's assistant.

"Anything wrong?" asks the girl with professional friendliness. You can tell. The difference between friendship like Sid's and the nurse kind of smile is the difference between getting paid and doing it for pleasure. And with this nurse,

55

it's obviously no pleasure. "Anything wrong?" she repeats.

"Of course something's wrong. Why else would I be here?"

Some people have to be put in their places. The way she'll have to do with Rose. But Rose is a widow, that's a mitigating circumstance. The nurse could be a widow, too. And so young!

Myra stands naked to the world as the doctor thumps away. If it weren't for Dr. Ackerman's scientific understanding, she'd never allow it. There's something about a man's touch which isn't right. Unless he's a husband, and you have to.

"Loss of appetite?"

"Never," she confesses.

"Worries?"

"None whatsoever."

"Pains?"

"Only when I think about them, Doctor Ackerman. Most of the time I'm too occupied to notice. You don't believe," Myra hesitates, "it could be change of life, do you?"

"Mrs. Russell, your menopause was fourteen years ago!"

Myra looks despondent.

"No," says Ackerman, his stethoscope tuned to her innermost secrets, "I'm afraid it's a very slight . . ."

He pauses. Myra looks him in the eye. "Yes?"

"Heart murmur," is the grim verdict. "No reason to be alarmed," as she collapses in a chair. "Main thing is to take it easy, relax, keep calm, don't rush, don't worry."

Myra Russell turns into a solid shaft of stone. He's prescribed the worst possible cure—a lifelong lull!

"Avoid tennis tournaments," he babbles sympathetically. "No handball, no weight-lifting, nothing strenuous."

She's got to get a grip on herself. She does *not* have a murmur and that's a fact. You can't expect a doctor to examine thousands of patients, year after year, without dreaming up something, or he'd be bored to death. Everyone has his own method of chasing away lulls and exaggeration is Dr. Ackerman's. She'll have to play along and seem anxious. "What about mental activity, Doctor?"

"You mean thinking? Nothing wrong with that."

"I mean chess. I'm afraid I'm in love with the game. Which could be quite strenuous. Because, you see, I have so many other organizations. SANITY, CHEMBAN, CONSERVE . . ."

"Excellent! Take your mind off things. Only don't get emotionally involved."

"Oh, I never get involved," explains Myra. "Of course I'm concerned. Who isn't, what with radioactivity and war and things. But I make it a cardinal rule never to worry. Or else I'd get so bogged down in one cause, I wouldn't find room for the others. That's how I manage to keep active. By not being overengrossed."

"Mrs. Russell, your heart murmur, I'm happy to say, is fairly slight."

Myra looks annoyed. As if she's spending her invaluable time and priceless money for nothing more than a bruise.

"Sixty, Mrs. Russell, is the dangerous age. You might call it the last lap in the race. If you want to cross that finish line in style, you've got to take it slow. That's why your husband never got there. Too many business worries."

57

Sixty, the dangerous age. What is she to do, stay home and knit? She doesn't have a grandchild to fret about. She doesn't have any saints to pray to like Rose. She doesn't have any hereditary enemies like Sid Tannenbaum. She doesn't have an image to forge like Victor. She doesn't even have a husband to fuss over like Debbie.

All she has is a restless heart. Murmur, nonsense! Her system's fine and dandy and she's going to go on believing that the rest of her days. Only the rest won't be long the way the world's going. The way they're poisoning the atmosphere, contaminating the water, adulterating the food. It makes her angry every time she thinks of it. No, she can't afford to think of it. She mustn't agitate her overworked blood stream. She must forget. Hurry, hurry, she completely forgot, CHEMBAN—she's late!

CHEMBAN isn't only a matter of life or death, CHEMBAN is fun:

"How many units of Strontium 90 in the milk you drank last month?"

"Ten."

"I say eight."

"I'll take a stab at fifteen."

"I'm on a diet," declares Myra. "I drink nothing but the powdered kind."

"Mrs. Russell, powdered milk only gets rid of the bad iodine. Against Strontium 90, it's no good at all."

"That's right, Mrs. Russell. Strontium 90's half-life is twenty-eight years."

"I always get mixed up on figures," says Myra. "Well,

58

let's take a guess. You say ten, you say eight and she says fifteen. Then I say . . ." Myra reflects: how many shares must she sell tomorrow just to stay alive? "Twenty."

"You win, Mrs. Russell! You see, fellow CHEMBANites, it doesn't pay to be too optimistic."

"Of course not," says Myra. "Considering what we're up against—the preservatives in our jams, the mothproofing in our clothes, the chemicals in our pastries. Why even the Bomb Treaty, which they say is guaranteed, could be repudiated at any moment."

"A rotten shame."

"It's enough to make you sick."

"Darn fools."

A most enjoyable evening. Compare it to Monday's SANITY, with its endless dissension. How can you insist on peace when your own group is at war? No, contention is not her cup of tea. When she lived with Ralph, her Golden Rule was never to argue. Once in a while, naturally, she'd hold a grudge. But raise the roof? Never. Rose wouldn't stand for it. And there's no replacing someone you've had for two decades. For that matter, there was no replacing Ralph. She refused to be like those other widows, changing husbands in midstream just because they were bored.

"Mrs. Russell, please!"

"Oh, sorry. My mind completely drifted."

"The prize, Mrs. Russell." He hands her a handsome book.

"*Your Poisoned Food: A Guide for the Unwary*. Just what I've always wanted," she mutters as she busily scans the index. Intriguing. Certainly more worthwhile than fiction. And if *Your Poisoned Food* proves too difficult, she can turn on educational television. What if there's nothing educational? That will mean two lulls, *Your Poisoned Food* and her color TV. A night of servitude, imprisoned between the dull sheets of insomnia. No, she mustn't! Last week she took too many of those strange pills. A slight mishap. Which is why her heart seems so persistent. She's got to pull herself together, extract herself from the doldrums, rejoin the quiz, America, the world.

"What's in bread that can shorten your life? The winner gets a jar of unsprayed Japanese honey."

Myra, searching her soul for a clue, is completely stumped.

❧

"Rose, what are you doing!"

"Looking over your books, Mrs. Russell. So I can give 'em a good dusting."

"Since when do you clean *behind* the books? And why at one A.M.?"

"Because I can't get to sleep with that TV of yours. Mary-Mother-of-Jesus, don't you ever go to bed? You been in a wake for two years, Mrs. Russell. What you need is a man. Only you don't have one so you blame me because I don't believe in being a widow. So you get jealous and yell at me for keeping your encyclopedias in order. It don't pay to be generous. It absolutely don't pay."

"Rose, you're absolutely right. Look what a mess tonight turned out to be. Sid insists if those Tyranny Tests begin again, we've got to take action. So Vic Brown accuses him of being a hothead. Then Kovski, whom I convinced into joining, says they're both nonlogical dreamers.

"Well, Rose, after the bickering, we finally got to see *The Horrors of Hate, Part I.* Literally, it gave me the chills. When the love scene came on, what do you think this ten-year-old director did? He refused, point blank, to show the heads. You didn't know who was the man and who was the woman. And they both had knives sticking in each other's back. You see, even though they were married, they truly hated each other and it was supposed to be symbolic. Sid said it was sheer genius. Vic said it was an oddity. Kovski wasn't even watching. He was trying to explain to me his new theory of world mismanagement. Only I couldn't look at him and still watch the haters on the screen. Real people, Rose. Not one false actor in the cast. Where are you going? Rose O'Connor, I'm not through. Don't leave. I'll go out of my mind! It's too late to call Debbie, the TV isn't working, the movie houses are all closed, and Dr. Ackerman refuses to give me more sleeping sickness pills. Because he says I'm too lax. Which is exactly my trouble. My heart! Rose, I can hear the murmur!"

Rose shoves back the atlas, flicks off the chandelier and slips out the door.

❧

She won't play cards again if it kills her! Forty dollars thrown out the window. More than an entire chess lesson. At least, at the King's Castle, she'd have sharpened her wits, her mind, her concentration, now so rapidly fading away.

No, she can't afford to be senile at fifty-nine. When D&K climbs back to its rightful place, she'll reinvest in something secure. Like the United States Government. Which, they claim at SANITY, is being undermined by missiles. Which are being turned out as fast as children in India. Which country, they say at CONTROL, will commit suicide if it doesn't pull itself together, like her, and get a grip on reality.

Maybe she'll begin tomorrow.

She glances at her new lapel watch. Guaranteed an entire year. Enough to carry her past sixty, the age of retirement, the age of leisure, the age of anguish. She pounds on Paul's eighteenth-century door.

A twentieth-century echo: "Hold your horses!"

She shouldn't be so dependent. Paul is twenty-nine, with a half-life of his own to waste. But since when is friendship with a son neurotic? Noticing a few unoccupied minutes in her bulging schedule, she just ran by for a hurried hello.

"Hello," she nods, entering without being asked. Young people! "Sybil dear, you're looking ghastly. Rings under your eyes. You've got to catch up on your sleep. Only don't take drugs. It's bad for one's memory. Paul dear, how's your work coming? You seem positively pooped. Don't either of you get enough shuteye?" Sex—that's their trouble! Demanding too much of each other. Look at them, a worn-out husband and a frustrated goat of a wife. "Eight full hours," she warns. "Anything less and it shows."

Staring at her haggard face, they hand her a limeade steeped in gin. Silently, they prop a goosedown pillow behind her blue-blonde head. A brand new shade. Designed to look young but not foolish. Thirty dollars a curl. The same price as Kovski's vicious offensive. But why analyze the price of an hour?

"Lovely, Mrs. Russell. That new pony tail is so unusual."

62

"Damn sewer lines," grumbles Paul, as he returns to his mysterious map. "They keep getting tangled up with the water main. And now the s.o.b.'s say no go on slab foundations. That means expensive basements. We'll have to cut down in other ways. Cheapen the siding, eliminate windows, hide the rubber plumbing behind some plasterboard walls."

"It's all too technical for me," says Myra, trying to unclog her straw. "Anyhow, be glad *you* have a nice home. Rafters, beams, real oak flooring. That's the way it goes. Yesterday's horse stable is today's luxurious living. But that's no reason to be pessimistic. The problem is as plain as the nose on Sybil's face. Too many people, that's the trouble."

"It's no trouble," says Paul, "it's a pleasure. Where we're building, just five years ago was nothing but trees. Sure, it's O.K. to join those organizations, Mom. Damn good outlet. Only don't take them seriously or you'll go batty."

"Paul's right, Mrs. Russell. Every cloud has its silver lining. The boom in population is his opportunity to sell more Happiness Homes."

"If those houses are so fine," says Myra, "then why don't you buy one?"

"You kidding, Mom? What would we do with three bedrooms?"

"Fill them," snaps Myra.

Sybil's mustache bristles. "Paul and I are too involved in our careers."

Instead of a child, another wagonwheel chandelier, a butter-churn floorlamp. Well, someone has to be penalized for other people's surplus. And why not the Russells?

Because she'd like to have grandchildren, that's why! Because she'd like to be welcomed, hugged, kissed. Because she doesn't want to end up a widow all her life.

Paul rolls up his map. "Only one more tract before we hit mountain. That's Everett White's place. Three hundred acres, flat as a pancake. We've got to make the Parklands Commissioner understand. 'Listen,' I'll tell him, 'it's people or parks. And frankly, I'll put my money on people. I'm for the voter, the man who pays for your job, the man who's clamoring for a cut-rate suburbia. If you gobble up the farm, you'll be evicting families from houses that aren't even built. We've got to take this population explosion seriously, D'Agostino. We're all in this boat together. And the boat's sinking because there're too damn many passengers. That means we gotta expand the boat. That means more Happiness Homes.'"

"Here's our latest Maisonette," says Sybil, enveloping her in an enormous two-and-a-half floorplan, which is nothing but a one-room, walk-in closet.

"I guess I could think it over. Only thinking is exactly my trouble. Yours, too. If you didn't think so much, you'd have had a child by now. And if I'd had a grandchild, I wouldn't have to be visiting you. And if I didn't have to be visiting you, I could have my grandchildren visit me. I could be reading them stories, taking them to lectures, concerts, childrens' museums. Buying them chemistry sets, ballet lessons. Improving their minds instead of . . ." She examines Sybil's earnest face. A face whose only interest is not humanity or the Bomb or those dyes on lemon peels . . . Myra stops sipping. Who knows: limes, too.

"More limeade, Mrs. Russell?"

"No, I'm afraid. I mean delicious, only I just remembered. I have an urgent meeting."

"Syb and I agree, they're great apartments, Mom. You ought to see the automatic garbage disposal and that electric dishwasher."

"I have Rose for dishes. And I've no intention of disposing of a devoted employee. Not as long as my stocks hold out. I am not moving into a Maisonette so I can be wretched all day because no one wants to visit."

Paul drops his map. Like the one missing from her atlas. Marked with arrows, crosses and exclamation marks. He hides it behind his back, looking like a little hurt puppy. She shouldn't have jumped to conclusions. Now he'll be so sensitive, she'll never be able to mention the loan. "G'bye," says Myra, briskly kissing his unshaven cheek.

Anyhow, maybe he'll do it without being asked. Half her remaining legacy. He'll use it to buy the last farm, cover it with houses, so he can make a fortune, so maybe he can repay. She slams the fragile door. With her finances, he *has* to repay, there's no maybe about it.

"And in conclusion," D'Agostino guzzles his mineral water, "the Department of Parklands owes no small debt to you who struggle that the precious forests and lakes and streams of our undefiled heritage, the heritage of our teeming cities, the heritage of our millions upon millions of descendants . . ."

Myra pictures the millions, swarming over the land like locusts. She must get an appointment to CONTROL's

Decoration Committee. Let that be her modest contribution to the cause of population. The Commissioner is saying something urgent. Back to taking notes. But it's so difficult when her mind keeps wandering. Sad thoughts: shares of D&K being sold for a song. Evil thoughts: Rose O'Connor, right this minute, escaping over a rainbow with Ralph's pot of plundered gold. Myra Russell, will you please pull yourself together and listen!

"One more word," intones the Commissioner. "Every tree chopped is a tree gone forever. Every acre bulldozed, is an acre gone forever. There must be houses, we of the Department don't deny that. But there must be parks as well, so that our region's increasing population, fifteen million today, one hundred million within our lifetime, that the hundred million residents of our bustling metropolis may dawdle beneath the hemlocks and recall what this country was like when it was an underdeveloped, savage wilderness. Before our great governor established the Department of Parklands. A department, members of CONSERVE, which needs your support in its drive to increase our inadequate, ridiculously impoverished salaries!"

Applause. That means higher taxes. Well, there's nothing more important than parks. Except, of course, peace. Her secretarial pencil scribbles *impoverished salaries*.

"In final conclusion, I shall do everything in my power to forestall the housing developers from gobbling up the Everett White farmstead."

But how can that be; Paul said they saw eye to eye!

"When, in the course of park conservation, it becomes

66

necessary to purchase, we shall purchase. When we are forced to condemn, we shall condemn. There's no need to stir up a hornet's nest by antagonizing our legislators. Leave it to the Department of Parklands. We shall do the job, and we shall do it well!"

Should she tell them, split the case wide open? But a man's innocent unless you can prove it. Maybe D'Agostino has decided to take the land for the people, the park system, for posterity after all. Her pencil takes down the words *do it well!*

"A last thought if you will bear with me. I have no intention of letting these three hundred acres fall into the hands of chiselers. I have no intention of letting these precious woodlands fall into the itchy fingers of speculators. Their axes are sharp. But ours are sharper. Their hunger for land is great. But ours is greater. Their eagerness to develop is enormous. But ours is even more enormous. Ladies and gentlemen of CONSERVE, I give you my sacred word as a lawyer and commissioner, the Last Forest shall not be bulldozed!"

The room fills with bravos. Myra joins in. Let Happiness Homes lose. Paul's a Harvard graduate and can find other employment. A park is a park. A thing of beauty. Priceless. Forever. A collection box in the shape of a tree trunk. Myra thrusts in a chlorophyll-colored bill.

Was that a ten! It's too late. Anyhow, it's for a good cause. The cause of trees, of grass, of birds. After all, what is money but the cause of unhappiness? If she had a thousand in her purse, she'd donate that. But she doesn't. Lord knows she doesn't have it. She must see her broker first thing tomorrow. That way, insisting, pleading, explaining, questioning, she can kill an entire morning's lull.

It's all in a day's work.

A day's work:

5:37 A.M. Rise and shine. Sun not shining. Better not to rise. Back to bed with Nembutal.

9:19 A.M. Before brushing teeth, peek into medicine cabinet for phantom bundle marked *treasure*. Gone!

10:34 A.M. The goldrush to Wall Street. "D&K, hurry, sell!" That hour, Danbury & Kent, New England's second oldest rail line, plunges off trestle to an all-time low.

11:03 A.M. Resisting broker's pleas to convert holdings to missiles, pesticides, baby foods, Myra cries "Never! A betrayal of SANITY, CHEMBAN, CONTROL . . ." That morning, missiles, pesticides and baby foods reach an all-time high.

12:10 P.M. Alex's condition grave. Debbie cancels luncheon. Forced to dine in solitary splendor at a table for two. A long, lousy lull. They're staring, asking why is that poor woman eating alone, doesn't she have any friends? Yes, hundreds! Myra glances up defiantly. Only they're home scrubbing floors, in factories punching clocks. Her friends are cooking, laundering, buying, selling, busy every miserable minute of every frantic day. Clutching her empty handbag, Myra rushes off to nowhere.

1:00 P.M. Standing on the street corner, she wonders what to do.

Stroll in Central Park: too many rapists.

Chess with Kovski: too expensive.

Telephone visit with Debbie: a waste of time.

Exhibition of abstract art: a waste of paint.

A fascinating book. A rented copy of that best-selling novel, *Troubles*, about the evils and glories of war. Something to distract her troubled mind. If only she can concentrate.

1:45 P.M. She can't. Rose's radio booms like an atomic explosion. The tingling of an imaginary phone. She races for the receiver: silence. The doorbell: no one. She keeps hearing, seeing, thinking things. What if her money gives out and she's thrown into the penniless streets? *I treasure . . .* What, Ralph darling? Finish the sentence, the prison sentence, the clue, the missing link, which, like that one in evolution, transformed them from the indignity of thoughtless animals into the majesty of tortured human beings. She'll concentrate on something else. Her one and only son.

2:22 P.M. "I would like to speak to Mr. Paul Russell. Tell him it's his mother." She stares at the pack of mentholated cigarettes. Mustn't pick up any of Rose's expensive habits. "Paul, it's me. Just wanted to hear your voice. Of course you're busy. Who isn't? The Last Forest! Well, I happen to have inside information that you're going to lose out. The Parkland Commissioner. Yes, he said over his dead body and not to worry. Why are you laughing? He says people are more important than Happiness. Paul, stop that giggling! You need a vacation. In the woods somewhere, to commune, to be alone. Like me. Paul dear, I suddenly remembered. I've got a meeting tonight. I must get Rose to defrost the dinner. Someday try dropping over. You haven't

69

visited in six months. Paul, Paul!" No answer, a total blank, as if the phone company, in exasperation, has cut her off. Myra slams down the deaf and dumb receiver.

"Rose, would you lower the radio so I can talk? What have you done with the telephone money, sweetheart? The money I gave to pay the bill. But I'm sure I did. Rose, I can't hear you over that gangster program."

Myra scans her bewildered checkbook. Where's the stub? She must have lost it. Now she's hurt poor Rose's feelings.

"Stop that crying, Rose. Yes, I'm sorry. I'll pay you again. This time I'll make absolutely sure."

Keep up this forgetfulness and soon there'll be no electricity. No television, no toast, no hair dryer. Then Rose. Then the weekly window washer. She'll be forced to pull down the shades. Her apartment will be as dark as a cave. All day long she'll sit in her Park Avenue tomb, a stone-age widow, waiting for the war clouds to gather.

Hurry, before she falls into a depression. She's got to grab a shower, climb into a smart new dress, rush into a cab, urge him to speed, just in time for a fun-filled, incredibly worthwhile evening.

Only where? Never mind, just hurry, hurry before her mind gets out of joint.

4:10 P.M. Defrosted *crêpes suzette*—one, two, three and away they go.

4:28 P.M. Automatic hydro-massage followed by Dandelion Hair Rinse.

5:55 P.M. Dandy hairdo wrapped in lavender towel.

6:04 P.M. Time out for treasure. The baseboard, the doorsill, the WELCOME mat. Foiled again.

6:05-7:59 P.M. Changing and rechanging of the hats, each a different personality. How should she seem today—peasant, pleasant, chic, slick, glittering or gilded? Casting off her sequined cloche, she decides to be simple.

8:15 P.M. *The Statistics of Destiny.* The CONTROLites sit in rapture as the professor expounds. A lull, like the droning of a headache. Only worse, because there's no drug can cure but fascination. And though the professor is talking about life and death, birth and rebirth, it certainly isn't fascinating.

"So, in conclusion . . ."

Those promising false words—*In conclusion, To summarize.* And then they go on and on.

"At the 1800 to 1850 growth rate, it took the world 135 years to double its population. At the 1900-1950 rate, doubling took 67 years. But at the current world growth rate, it will require only 42 years."

Myra converts the pleasant abstractions into bitter reality. The city will be transformed into one big Maisonette. Happiness Homes, instead of nestling on half-acre estates, will squat on quarter-, eighth-, sixteenth-acre lots. Touching each other, on top of one another, squeezing each other like perverted lovers. Sybil and Paul will join forces. As the rooms grow smaller, Happiness-Maisonettes will expand. Half-room apartments, quarter-, eighth-rooms . . .

"If the present rate continues, in 200 years the world will have 50 billion people. Now this is the absolute maximum our planet can support. And to my mind, that's a terribly optimistic estimate."

What's so optimistic about 50 billion! A hasty calculation. Seventeen times more people than today. Think of the jammed subways, the difficulty in catching a cab. Think of department stores, phone booths, elevators seventeen times more packed. Think of seventeen Times Squares condensed into one. Though at least it's more interesting than the suburbs where there's nothing to do. But with seventeen times more people, there won't even be suburbs!

The women of CONTROL are aroused to indignation.

"In 800 years," continues the learned statistician, "not a very long time as time goes . . ."

Sounds long to her. But she must get a grip on herself, the historical view. She must forget her onrushing sixtieth birthday, Rose's demand for back pay, Paul's demand for another loan, SANITY's demand for higher dues. She must wipe away all trivial concerns and concentrate on the larger issues. Maybe, lending an ear, she'll learn of a solution to her own petty, but pressing situation.

"Inside 800 years, the earth will have a population of one person for every square foot of land. That includes mountains, volcanos, glaciers, deserts. One person per square foot!"

And she thought she had problems. Exclamations, gasps of *awful*, murmurs of *incredible!* A lovely hat. Probably one of a kind. That's what she likes about CONTROL: it's so high-toned.

"Let's get down to facts."

Yes, let's.

"Underprivileged people can indulge freely in but one pleasure: sexual intercourse . . ."

In this day and age, why be prudish? Because she's past

her prime, that's why. Because her youth is spent, her days are numbered, and she's got to be realistic.

"We of CONTROL's Research Bureau must find pleasures which are equally powerful . . ."

Other pleasures: there's chess, there's art, there's community welfare. A thousand chaste and worthwhile pleasures.

"We must make the peasants comprehend the onus of too many offspring. We must force them to be concerned for their starving families. We must, in a nutshell, give the indifferent masses of Asia, Africa and Latin America something to worry about."

Myra looks worried.

10:45 P.M. "I recommend," says Mrs. Benedikt, "that every costume for the Contrillion be approved by our board. Remember last year's bare-as-a-button Adam and Eve?"

"Excuse me, Mrs. Benedikt." It's Myra in a rare personal appearance. "But you haven't decided about the Decoration Committee. Without making a campaign speech, I'd like very much to be elected. I feel if there's anyone who has time for decorations, it's me."

Mrs. Benedikt's eyes turn to ice. "My dear Mrs. Russell, we appreciate your keen interest, but the selection of officers is not on this week's agenda. To continue," she turns to the others, "the Fund-Raising Committee suggests we organize a tour of prominent New York houses."

Why not? There's nothing in the world wrong with Altman Chippendale. Her apartment raising money for a noble cause. CONTROL's socialites admiring her late-Victorian din-

73

ing room, her remaining Apostle crockery, gaping at her wrought-iron settee.

"Meeting adjourned!"

Praise be.

11:08 P.M. "Nice evening, huh?"

"Park Avenue and seventy-ninth."

"Hope they can keep it up. A few more games like that and they'll win for sure."

"The things I went through tonight, Mr. . . . Callahan. If it goes on, we'll all be living in Maisonettes. Look at me with a giant living room and a huge den and a breakfast nook and two great big bedrooms. In fifty years, I'll be lucky to have room for even a cot. In a hundred, I probably won't even have a place to stand."

"In a hundred years, sweetheart, none of us'll be standing."

"Exactly. Of course we have to accept it. Progress, I mean. To fight the future is to fight progress. It's all in Divine Technology."

"You can't fight City Hall, sweetie."

"You certainly can't, Mr. Callahan. It's so perplexing, this CONTROL affair. Sometimes I wonder if I sat back and took it easy, wouldn't things solve themselves."

"Listen, little people like us don't stand a chance. The other day, I took my wife and eight kids . . ."

"Eight!"

"Sure. Five girls and three boys. Wanta see their pictures?"

"Eight children, that's exactly what I'm talking about."

"Somethin' wrong with raising a family?"

74

"Nothing at all. I have one myself. A handsome young son. He's out to make a name for himself in real estate. Happiness Homes."

"Hey, I seen them. Pretty fancy for economy colonies. Trouble is the school taxes. Too rich for my blood."

"And do you know why school taxes are so high, Mr. Callahan?"

"Graft."

"Children. A surplus. In five hundred years, there'll only be one square inch for every living person alive."

"Thank the saints I won't be around then."

"But your eight children will be."

"You kidding? Five hundred years from now?"

"Well, then, your sixty-four grandchildren. Or your four thousand great-grandchildren. Or your sixteen million great-great grandchildren. You've got to control yourself, Mr. Callahan, I can't multiply any higher. You can see it isn't fair for everyone to keep on like this. Haven't you heard of birth control?"

"That'll be two-seventy, lady," slamming to a stop.

"Outrageous!"

"What d'you expect? 179th Street's halfway to Westchester."

"But I said *seventy*-ninth."

"You do so much talking, you don't pay attention. Trouble with you, sweetheart," he wheels the taxi around, "you got too many worries. Why don't you relax once in a while? Try sitting back and stop aggravating."

"Maybe I will," says Myra. "Yes, maybe I will. But of course the birth problem isn't the only . . ."

11:41 P.M. How to spend the few remaining minutes? An all-night movie. A double feature, to last longer. Yes, a duet of tender love stories with old-fashioned, happy endings. That way, immersed in the dark, she'll lose herself in someone else's troubles.

Alone on her bed, Myra gazes at the vacant pillow beside her as she waits for the drugs to take hold. A blurred vision: Debbie busily tending her ailing hubby; Rose praying excitedly to some glamorous saints; Paul building papier-mâché houses; Sybil renting apartment cubicles; Dr. Ackerman being paged for emergency operations. That thump of her murmuring, economy-model heart, warning her to concentrate on tomorrow, to organize every spare second, to bury herself in an orgy of diversion.

The cuckoo clock crows midnight. Day is done.

❧

Myra glares at her crossword puzzle, trying to piece things together. For the third time she consults her unabridged dictionary. "Premise of a Syllogism in eight vertical letters." As mysterious as Ralph's last words. *High treasure* . . . his finger pointing like the hand of God. Then blackout, a murder mystery, the film snapping just when they were about to announce the killer. If only she hadn't upset his nerves with that modish grapefruit. Which caused the debacle. Which caused the film to break, Ralph to collapse, the treasure to dissolve, herself to be buried in budgets, bonds and emptied bankbooks. And now D&K zooming downhill, the airbrakes gone, the conductor vanished, a railroad with thousands of screaming widows, rushing headlong into the valley of insolvency.

"Happy Mother's Day, Mrs. Russell," handing Myra a gorgeous bouquet.

"Rose! But this must have cost a fortune."

"It's all right, I took it out of the grocery money!"

"What are we going to eat next week, flowers?"

"Mrs. Russell, some people are so stingy it hurts. Cheer them up when their own children forget, and they hide behind a fake budget. First, no flowers. Then, no Rose O'Connor. Well, who's going to make your toast for you, answer me that. And give out the laundry? And defrost your dinners?"

"Rose, you're absolutely right. Could you tell me what's a KIWI in fourteen letters?"

"Mrs. Russell, just because I used household money on flowers, don't mean it's not a present. Ever since your husband died, you been tighter than a Jew."

"Please, Rose, be tolerant. It's that railroad, dear. Every time I sell a share, it's like stealing a locomotive. The D&K and I are *both* in trouble. What's a fool in two letters?" Awful to change subjects in midstream. But you can't always be worrying about important problems. If CONTROLites thought only of the population catastrophe and didn't fret about their annual ball once in a while, they'd all have ulcers.

"A fool in two letters, Mrs. Russell, is me."

Rose marches back to her tiny bedroom. There'll be no housecleaning today, poor thing. Super-sensitive. She wonders if Paul has totally forgotten. Now that she's a widow, he probably doesn't think of her as a mother any more. But then he's married and she still thinks of him as a son. That's because she's old-fashioned. She must modernize.

$E = MC^2$. Which means there's no room for sentiment: Mother's Day, Father's Day are things of the past. So are birthdays. They'll probably forget her sixtieth. Which means she can, too. By engrossing herself with worthwhile lectures and worthy causes, she'll forget all about growing old. She'll be too busy to recall what day it is, what month, what year it is. Who knows, maybe time itself will disappear.

The doorbell. Her son. She's a mother after all!

"Oh, Debbie. I thought it was . . ."

"Roses!" exclaims Mrs. Hilliard. "How extravagant of Paul."

Myra lays down her insoluble crossword puzzle. Why wrack your brains when you can get the answer in tomorrow's paper?

"It's holidays like this that make me wonder why I never had a child," says Debbie, treating herself to a nonfattening chocolate. "But then your children leave you, your husband leaves you, and what do you end up—a widow."

"It's not so bad," says Myra, grimly. "You don't want dinner at six, you take it at seven. You don't care to wake up at dawn, you wake up at noon. No more responsibilities. No more commitments."

"And no more entangling alliances," continues Debbie, helping herself to another. "No one to yell at you, no one to apologize to. Freedom, that's the most important thing in life."

"I quite agree," says Myra, deciding to forget about a four-letter synonym for love, to sit back and endure Debbie's endless visit. "When Ralph used to live with me, I was always so concerned: was he coming home on time, would he put up with another avocado pie, would he take me to another hit show. Now I'm independent. I don't care who likes avocado. If I want to see a hit show, I don't ask any more. Who is there to ask? I just go alone and try to enjoy it."

"Casablanca," Debbie goes on, "Greece, the pyramids. When Alex leaves, I'm going to take my mind off his final departure with a marvelous itinerary. Of course I'll have regrets. Not having a child will mean no stunning flowers on Mother's Day."

"These roses are nothing," sniffs Myra. "Paul does it all the time."

"But then, if I had a son, I'd have a million worries. Will his new wife be more attractive than I am? How many children should they have?" looking Myra in the eye. "How many times a week should they visit? This way, I'm truly free. No one to worry about except little me."

"You have a point there," confides Myra.

"Got to go," says Debbie. "Alex is due for a transfusion. That means a brand-new nurse. With my husband in a delirium, I could be disinherited at the drop of a hat."

"Don't let it happen!" Myra cries out. "No matter what. Without money, what's the use of being a widow?"

"Look who's talking. How many D&K's did you dump this week? Why, Alex told me confidentially, you ought to *enlarge* your holdings. At today's bargain prices you could make a killing." Debbie reaches for a departing nougat.

"A killing," repeats Myra, as the door slams *goodbye*.

79

Before long, there'll be nothing to kill, no more shares to murder. She'll have years of time and not a speck of money. What a nightmare!

Hunting for an unforgettable movie, Myra opens to her latest *Happenings-The Guide for Stepping Out*. No, that's last week's. She rummages through her recent magazines: *Sanity Revue*, *Mansions Beautiful*, *Love*, *Truth*, *Time*. Subscription dreams, Debbie calls them. Well, it's easier to live in a dreamhouse mansion than to pay off an overdue mortgage, easier to read about Time than to know what to do with it, easier to love Truth than to find true Love.

Bedroom Incident. She's seen it. Anyhow, it's too idealistic. *The Mating Nest*. She's seen that one, too. Weren't they wise not to marry. *The Cattle Rustlers*. She can't stand guns. *Midnight Ravens*. No, she must confine herself to four-star, rave-review features.

Theatrical Amusements page. Only Broadway's closed tighter than a casket; actors need a day off, too. A day off from what? A day off from responsibilities, that's what. A day off from pressing problems, from urgent meetings, a day off from social commitments.

It's Mother's Day and either she treats herself to something interesting, inexpensive and enjoyable or she might as well be childless like Debbie or sterile like Sybil or just plain crazy like Rose. Which, dear God, she is not and never will be, if only she can keep her mind fascinated.

❧

The King's Castle lies deserted. They're all out visiting their mothers. If only hers were alive, a place to go, something to do. But her relatives are either dead or in Los Angeles. At fifty-nine (almost sixty!), it's too late suddenly to pull up roots. Anyhow, Rose hates Southern California. You can't dismiss a loyal domestic that easily. Nor can you begrudge a disloyal son because he imagines Mother's Day is next week. These days, how can anyone keep track? Which reminds her of the railroad with its crumbling, termite-ridden roadbeds.

"Business is miserable," mutters Kovski. "In America, they'd rather do crossword puzzles." Myra looks at him guiltily. "Sit. I'll play you a game. We'll talk, drink coffee. Maybe you'll learn."

Igor's first move. A pawn, the same as last week. It's the Serf Defense, the defense that's really an attack. She must be on her toes. If she loses once again, he'll become discouraged.

"I'm doing research," mutters Kovski as he snatches her pawn. "On behalf of the movement. And would you like to know my final conclusion?"

Myra's queen tiptoes back. Just in time. "What's that, Igor?" He's trying to lead her astray, take her mind off the battle. She'll simply have to concentrate. She'll crawl in stealthily while he chats about peace. Then she'll strike, butchering them one by one.

No, a woman shouldn't allow a man to lose his self-esteem. She'll let Kovski win. But inside, she'll know she was truly the better man. She's all confused. Whose turn? Better not ask. Ask and he'll charge for a lesson.

"Conclusion number one: the only way to have peace is world government. Conclusion number two: the only way to have world government is an equal balance of powers. Conclusion three: the only way to have equal balance . . ."

Mustn't listen. Mustn't be diverted. Even though she'll throw the game because she's a good sport doesn't mean she has to lose badly. Beware of the Serf Defense suddenly turning on her, pawns circling, horses cantering, bishops crucifying.

". . . impossible to have an equal balance of power without some fool upsetting the apple cart. Just one lonely aviator too bored to question, one tin general too neurotic to judge can destroy, single-handedly, our entire civilization."

"And believe you me, there are plenty of that type around," says Myra, looking up from the smoke of battle. "My friend, Debbie, is an excellent example. Sybil, too. She and my son, Paul, are having a contest to see who can sell more bad housing. They're all full of neuroses. Whose move?" Now she's done it! He'll turn it into a lesson. Thirty dollars per.

"The white moves after the black, Mrs. Russell. And since I'm black, and since I just moved my knight, and since you're white, it's your move."

For such an extremely long answer, he'll surely charge. Myra is beside herself. There's only one dollar and fifty cents to her name. She'll ask to open a charge account. The way she does in better department stores.

"I'm going to report that my researches have led to one conclusion: there is no solution. The conflagration is inevitable. Checkmate!" Myra's handbag drops to the floor. "In the first ten moves of chess, Mrs. Russell, there are 169,518,829,100,544,000,000,000,000 different possibilities. But in the next ten years, the possibilities of avoiding nuclear disaster are, I'm convinced, zero."

"Awful," shrugs Myra. "Well, guess I'll run along," she announces cheerfully. "Let's see, the bill comes to . . ."

"Thirty . . ." she holds her breath, "cents," declares Kovski.

Think of it! He could have called it a lesson and he merely charged for a game. That's why he's so discouraged. Well, he who doesn't ask, doesn't get. It's Mother's Day and she's got to be affirmative. Not like poor Mr. Kovski. It's Mother's Day and she's going to see her son. Invitation or no invitation, win or lose, do or die, neither rain, nor snow, nor gloom of day can stop her appointed rounds.

As Mother Russell enters the chic horse barn, Paul is shouting into his early-American telephone:

"If the Commissioner gets tough, we'll find some other place. When there's no more cornfields, we'll chop down the trees. When there's no more trees, we'll fill in the swamps. When the swamps are all filled . . ."

"Sit down," whispers Sybil. "Paul will be through in a minute."

Myra squats on a three-legged milking stool.

". . . then we'll drain the lakes. When the lakes are all dry, we'll level the hills. When everything's leveled and chopped and drained, hell, we'll buy a new zoning ordinance and build on the front lawns. And when there's no more lawns, then we'll wipe out the back yards. And when the houses are touching each other and it looks like the jig's up, we'll just tear 'em down and start all over again. Only this time, we'll build higher. Twenty, forty, sixty stories, the sky's the limit."

Myra indulges in a chocolate-covered cherry. Lucky for her Dr. Ackerman isn't there to say no. After all, you only live once. Which is plenty.

"Don't worry, pal. Old man White will sell or my name isn't Russell. I'm driving there today. And don't blow your brains out over Commissioner D'Agostino. Listen, nothing can stop Happiness. Because housing's just as big a racket as defense and don't you forget it!" Paul slams the receiver. "Mom, how's the kid?"

"Couldn't be nicer," shrugs Myra, depositing the pit in a pre-Colonial butter churn. "Only why are you so stirred up on Sundays? This Sunday especially."

There! She's done everything possible. If he doesn't remember, it's because he's too busy making ends meet. Wearing himself out every day, supporting his wife's antiques; wearing himself out every night, supporting her frustrated whims.

"Let's get going," commands Sybil, filing away her index cards: the bachelors, old-maids, widows. The lonely, the deserted, the forgotten.

"Paul," says Myra, as he shoves her through the narrow threshold, "I don't want you to be disappointed if D'Agostino changes his mind. I heard him tell CONSERVE that the White farm is never going to be bulldozed."

"That's right, Mom," grunts Paul as yesteryear's Duesenberg sputters and sparks into life. "We don't use bulldozers any more, we use a new machine called the . . ."

"Don't forget to signal," interrupts Sybil. "Remember,

84

these are Sunday drivers."

"Sunday," repeats Myra, knowing that they're coming close, that it's on the tip of their busy tongues.

"Hold tight," orders Paul, as the Duesenberg charges down the highway in a blaze of nuts, bolts and pistons.

The Russells wend their merry way over graded hills and filled-in bogs, past lawnside Madonnas and roadside rests, over asphalted trails and toll-shack lanes. Past smog-strangled urbia, suburbia, superbia, past parceled plot and crowded graveyard, to civilization's latest border, a corn-field marked ACREAGE. And over it, an ominous SOLD!

She'd like to deliver a lecture from CONSERVE. Only it's Mother's Day, it's spring, it's her son. Why stir up trouble?

They pause at the corrugated mailbox: E. White. An old-fashioned farmer. Like Sybil with her hand-carved door-ways and her Manhattan stable. But being old-fashioned is so expensive today. Look at her, with an old-fashioned maid, an old-fashioned railroad, an old-fashioned six-room apart-ment.

The trio heads for the ramshackle homestead. Where, it's rumored, George Washington once napped. Well, patriot-ism isn't everything. There's such a thing as cooperation. Now it's Everett White's turn to modernize. Just as, soon, it will be her turn. Sybil's, too. Technology. She wonders when they'll raise the DT fee.

Past the old-fashioned milk shed, the old-fashioned silo, the old-fashioned chickens, cows, even horses. They knock on the old-fashioned door. Everett White, old-fashioned and crotchety, peers out the crack.

85

"Here again," smiles Paul. "I got them to give a concession, a Happiness Home all paid for and decorated." He pats Mr. White's bony spine. "An end to all your problems. Never mind the cows waking you or the roosters croaking so you can sell their eggs. Never mind looking at the sky and worrying is there too little rain, too much sun? Just set the sprinkler and forget it. Wait till you see that nifty lawn. A full quarter-acre. Only you'll have to keep it up. Remember, you'll have neighbors now. A great gang of people. And the house, Mr. White, a real beauty. Split-Colonial."

"To kind of go with your personality," adds Sybil.

"No more running to the well every morning," says Paul. "Chrome faucets. And wait till you see the tile bathtub, the plaid dishwasher, the plastic toilet. Heck, that contraption in back of your house is a disgrace."

"Substandard," mutters Sybil, her nose in the air.

"And suppose, Everett, you decide to get married. An old codger like you probably still got plenty of life in him. Expandable attics, a few partitions and overnight you have yourself a six-bedroomer. That's why we call them Happiness Homes. Because they're equipped to handle all the happiness a guy can create.

"Well, Ev, you know the dough we're offering. And we think it's a damn good deal. Wait too long and you'll find the Parkland Commission buying you out at condemnation prices. Sell now, and you're set for life."

Poor Mr. White is exactly in her shoes. A male widow. Except he's got to work morning, noon and night. Well, she works, too. The same goal, but different methods. His way of spending time is farming—out-dated and old-fashioned.

86

Hers are lectures, meetings, protests—up-to-date and educational.

"When I was a boy . . ." It's the tongue-tied farmer. The Russells stare at him, a rare animal in a zoo. "Used to see deer coming out of those woods. Winters, they'd feed out of your hand. Woods used to be full of quail."

"Fascinating."

"Used to go to town on a horse. Used to drive a sleigh when the snow were deep enough. Used to hew my own wood."

"Just like a museum."

"Used to grow all my own food here. Potatoes, corn, beans."

How unbalanced! But free from chemicals.

"Had a bee hive, too. Used to tap the maples over there."

Real maple syrup. He's making her so hungry, she'd like to buy some. But Paul would get angry. They came to buy land, not sweets.

"Them days we used to have kerosene lanterns, rain-barrels, icehouses. Used to walk in the woods. Miles and miles. So far you could walk all day and you'd never reach the end. Beaver, muskrat, 'coons. And trees. Miles and miles and miles . . ."

Look at Paul, his mouth ajar, his eyes blazing like a well-lit development. "So terribly interesting," nods Myra. "I mean the history you gave." The old-fashioned farmer stares at them as if they're strangers. Then turns and walks away.

"Leave him alone," whispers Paul. "The poor fella wants to take one last look."

"A sentimentalist," says Sybil. "Like me."

87

"Who isn't?" sighs Myra.

"I told him a hundred times," mutters Paul. "Like it or not, Mr. White, there's no one in this world can stop the future. Because the future, well, it's like religion. You just gotta have it."

"You certainly do," says Myra. "And it's certainly been a most entertaining Mother's Day."

"Gee!" exclaims Paul. "I clean forgot. Congratulations, Mom!"

～✒

"Silver or gold?"

"Which one's better?" she asks, her mouth open to a yawn.

"Gold's better, silver's cheaper," mutters the dentist.

"How much better?"

"Gold will last forever. Silver, count on five, ten years."

Fifty-nine plus ten years makes sixty-nine. But her expectancy is seventy-two point seven.

"Yes?" The dentist's drill pauses impatiently.

"I'm thinking it over," she says. "I mean it's a philosophical question. You see, my income is limited and I don't want to throw it out on something temporary. I want a good, solid filling. But forever is such a long time." A momentary lull as she sits bogged in her insoluble dilemma. Yes, that's what hell must be, forever and a day with nothing to do. Myra brightens up. "I'll take the temporary," she concludes, "silver."

"Open," commands the dentist.

Her jaws part, ready for the sudden jab, the searing gouge, the insufferable roar. A strange way to spend an afternoon. Temporary. But then, when she's in her seventies and her schedule has ground to a total standstill, maybe she'll occupy her day by returning for a refill.

~∾

The Show Biz Cafe. Outdoor dining is a perfect solution to the pressing problem of leisure. Not that she doesn't have other problems. The problem of the Serf Defense. The problem of birds; the problem of bombs. The problem of too many problems. "Tea," she tells the black-stockinged waitress. "And, when you have the time, some pastries."

When you have the time. Foolish phrase. As if that waitress doesn't have all the time in the world. Lucky her.

Myra fumbles for the booklet in her purse. Something to while away the afternoon. *Our Disappearing Earth.* About erosion, corrosion, prostitution. As Vic Brown always says, what about just living? But then he's in public relations where you *have* to look content.

How pleasant it would be to sip tea with Tannenbaum as they planned a protest. But he's too busy forging anniversary charms, engagement rings, wedding bands, extracting money from other people's woes. If only she could be sipping with Kovski. But Igor is busy charging thirty dollars an hour, cents when he's cheerful. If only she could sip her Earl Gray with Rose. But Rose would say it's like being a call girl, sitting in an out-of-doors cafe, showing everyone you don't have a person in the world to share your tea, your conversation, your life with.

Rose is right. She should get up and leave this instant. Let's face it, leisure simply isn't her style.

Maybe, someday, she'll find a kindred soul. Why, there must be a million widows just like her, with time on their hands, with lulls around their necks, binding them to pots of cold tea, to gloomy pamphlets, to eroded planets.

Thoughtful and therefore depressed, Myra peers into her starved purse, and leaves the waitress an unforgiveably generous bribe.

∾

Myra has the blues. The endless day, scarcely begun, is turning into a prolonged lull. Or is she blue because of the lull, because she can't dream up a way to fill those empty, colorbook hours of hers?

She pauses at a red light, meditating beside a golden trash barrel. Which came first, the chicken or the egg, the lulls or the blues?

Orange. Ready, get set . . . Green and go! She races across the nameless asphalt stretch.

∾

Maybe, when Happiness succeeds, when the money rolls in, when the profits are counted, Paul will share the wealth. Meanwhile, she's got to pull in her belt, now stretched to the breaking point, and reduce expenses.

Rose and Myra step inside. A second step and they'll be out the window.

"Our latest Maisonette," explains Sybil. "The two-and-a-half."

"I only see one," snaps Rose.

Myra opens the door to the broom closet.

"The living room," Sybil thrusts out her thumb. "The

90

kitchenette," holding up a forefinger. "The bathroomette," holding out her pinky. "Two-and-a-half."

"What about the bedroomette?" asks Rose. "Or do I sleep in the bathtub?"

"Separate sleeping quarters are passé, Miss O'Connor. Especially in a crowded metropolis. That's why, in the model apartment, we use electronics. Press a button and the couch turns into a studio bed."

"Remarkable," says Myra, avoiding Rose's stern gaze. "But after all," she concedes, "it's progress, a technical advance, an inevitability."

"What happens if you're used to sleeping on a plain, unbuttoned bed and you're too old to change?"

"I suppose we've got to keep up with the times," says Myra, wondering what she'll do with her furniture. Put it in storage. But that costs money, too. Everything costs money. Breathing air-conditioned air costs money. Walking the street, wearing out shoe leather costs money. Even sitting home costs money: the high cost of upholstery, the price of a new rocker, the bill for repairing her colorless TV. And dying costs money, too. A tasteful casket, an uncramped burial plot, a well-meaning eulogy from a sincere, but expensive, minister.

"In these nerve-wracking times, Miss O'Connor," Sybil concentrates on the tougher customer, "you've got to improvise. If you need privacy, use a folding screen. If you need space, get a mirror. Trees, use mural wallpaper. Splendor? A reproduction chandelier. If you're old-fashioned and miss having windows, install a *trompe d'oeil* drapery."

"Mrs. Russell and me don't need any trumped oils, long as we got six rooms of our own."

"Anyway, it's *trompe l'oeil*," shrugs Myra.

"But Mother can't afford that oversized apartment," cries Sybil. "You're being very selfish."

"Selfish! Well, if you're in such a stew about Mrs. Russell's pocketbook, why don't you make that husband of yours pay back the loan?"

"Rose!" gasps Myra, wondering if she has a point.

"And if you think this cubbyhole is so darn great, how come you live in that swank townhouse? Why don't you move here, too? Why don't you buy one of Paul's cardboard houses?"

Myra tries to look stern. "We're here to examine the Maisonette, not find fault with an ambitious son."

"I'll admit Paul's developments aren't the best," concedes Sybil. "Why should they be? In twenty, thirty years, they'll be replaced by Maisonettes. And Maisonettes are not what I'd personally care for. But you see, Miss O'Connor, Paul and I happen to reside in an historic home, the original Vanderbilt stable. If we didn't live there, it would be sold to a speculator. We're simply trying to preserve a little history so that New York will be a more exciting place to live. You wouldn't want the whole city to be filled with Maisonettes, would you?"

"I've got work to do," frowns Rose, as the plastic doorhandle twists off into her hand.

"And I need more time to think it over," sighs Myra, wondering if she'll get Rose to climb onto the Maisonette ledge and wash that sooty fifty-ninth floor picture window without threatening to jump.

"No need to think. Just sign
In ink upon the dotted line."

A swansong from Sybil as she unrolls a handsome scroll engraved LIFELONG LEASE.

"Sign," warns Rose, jabbing the hallway button, "and you've lost your only friend in the world."

Myra's reply is drowned by the cheerful recorded music of the automatic elevator.

❧

Rose is searching for dust. Gold dust. The smug Chinese portraits are being lowered from the wall. She must have cleaned there ten times this month. Or was it last month? Ought to buy a calendar clock. The old one, an heirloom for generations, has sounded its last alarm. Everything breaking to pieces: her economy watch, her crippled heart, her color TV. And now the living room carpet. Rose must have dropped a stray cigarette. While humming torch songs to some imaginary boyfriend. Dare mention it and the poor girl will turn to tears.

But it could have been a hundred other people. Paul? He hasn't visited for months. And Debbie rarely smokes. So it must be Rose. Anyhow, now she can try out a new one: Persian, Kurdistan, Aubusson—why be a miser?

D&K, that's why! 8½ down ½. She'll have to visit Alex on his deathbed, explain her lapse of faith, beg him for a dying word of advice. Not treasure, *try sure*—that's what Ralph started to say.

93

Which meant, one—be sure to consult Alex, the manager of her estate; two—*try* to make him divulge a lucky tip, a stock which will soar to a new high, a stock which will save the day, now turned to night. The treasure chest gleaming before her, Myra flings open the subscription dream marked *Vacation Holidays.*

The French Chateau Junket. Why be confined to France, where the language is so difficult? *The Holy Land Tour.* Probably just Jews and Baptists. *The Iberian Package.* Guitars, gypsies, that's more her style. *Arctic Adventure for the Unadventurous.* Oh, for a glimpse of that scintillating midnight sun. Then there's India, Bali, Hawaii, Bolivia.

And what about her six-room apartment? When she returns from her years of adventure, a hardened and homeless sightseer, what will await her? A Maisonette, that's what.

And her social commitments? What will she say to the members when they hear she's run out on them?

She'll explain she's been doing research, accumulating data on Spanish birth control, investigating methods in Pakistan. A whole lifetime buried in science, every minute so enticing she can hardly wait for the sun to rise. And in the Arctic she won't even have to wait. Twenty-four hours a day devoted to a selfless and fascinating cause:

Myra Russell? You'll find her with her microscope, up there on the hill. Better hurry. Tomorrow she's off to Ceylon. There's never enough time for energetic little Mrs. Russell, the most interesting person I know.

Yes, come in. Please be careful where you step. I don't want you crushing any insects. Reverence for life and all that. It's part of my new conservation scheme. You'll have to sit on that stack of magazines. Articles I've written on how to find peace. Oh, I see you're reading my latest novel. Yes, wasn't it exciting? Excuse me while I take another look into my spectroscope. You see, I'm on the verge of a new discovery. An incredible, fantastic, unbelievable . . .

Myra sinks into a troubled stupor. The smile vanishes. The stout arms tremble. A nightmare. Sneak thieves. Ralph's secret treasure. Vanished! Now she's abandoned, widowed, standing in front of Sybil's renovated manger. No, she'll not ask for help like a worthless beggar. She'll stand there and wait, hoping Paul will take notice. All day long, all night long. Next morning they discover her proud corpse, stiff as a frozen leg of lamb.

Why didn't she knock? Why didn't she at least ask? She merely had to hold out her hand, and Paul would have come running with a bagful of lucre.

"Wake up, Mrs. Russell! Wake up! You told me to rouse you at dawn." Myra peers at Rose through bleary retinas. "Holy Infant-of-Prague, I can see you took those darn pills again. Remember that ticker of yours, Mrs. Russell. If you don't stop doping yourself up, you're headed for Kingdom Come."

"Hurry!" blurts Myra, barely able to walk, to see, to remember where she is, what time it is, who she is. "Hand me my picket sign, Rose. I'm going to protest!"

The Village called Greenwich jumps for joy. Tourists burst with boredom. Children threaten to become delinquent. Teen-agers, milling in front of jaded jazz joints, poetic pizza palaces, smother their lulls in platters of French fries. Middle-agers, too stout to French fry, too weary to jive, stroll down the maimed avenue, wondering what to do. Old people, too old to work, too rugged to die, search among the sightseers for a nonexistent bench. It's Sunday. The nation is in the throes of a lull. Sun-baked thousands loll on the beachheads. Movie-house millions stare vacantly as bored desperadoes riddle their lulls with bullets. In Congress, now adjourned, an indifferent janitor takes the chair. And the President. Papers signed, speeches delivered, nothing to do but gaze at that ominous atomic switch . . .

Lulls: the cause of wars, the cause of divorce, the cause of crime, the cause of sex, the cause of art, the cause which must be preserved at all costs. Hurry, hurry. Myra races down the boulevard, her arms burdened with petitions, placards, pickets. Hurry, before it's too late, before a restless President reaches for his button and the Constitutional Right-to-Lull is shattered forever.

Rumors, like storm warnings in a season of disenchantment: the Test Ban will be broken; the break will feature outer-space explosions; the explosions are necessary to find a cure for war; the cure will be so uncontrollable no nation will dare to use it.

Which sounds fine and dandy. But Sid Tannenbaum explains she's all wet. And Igor Kovski says they're both wrong, peace is insoluble. And Vic Brown says they've got to hustle more signatures. And Myra Russell says: "Have to

run now. Meeting of KOOLIE. Splendid cause. Life or death."
And flees into the teeming city.

She arrives at headquarters. KOOLIE, and underneath, the photo of a flightless bird. Flightless bird, that's it! KIWI in fourteen horizontal letters! Myra tugs at the bolted door. An awful mistake. It's Friday, CONTROL day, hurry, she'll be late for roll call!

The CONTROLers, thin-lipped and well-dressed, cluster about their mother hen, Penny Benedikt, as she raises her august fingers. "We've chosen the date for our Contrillion." She fishes in her petit-point purse. "The fourth day of July."

"Sacrilegious," cries Myra. "It's the day of my other protest." The women raise their dowager eyes. "I mean the Bomb has an intimate connection with our problem. Or so I'm told. It's because there are more people than jobs, more people than food or apartments. All that makes everyone restless. And restlessness leads to war. So you see, there's a relation. And that relation should be cemented. What I mean is, why don't we join SANITY in *their* march on Washington?"

"And cancel our cotillion?"

"And lose our integrity!"

"Mrs. Russell, we appreciate the fact that you belong to other organizations," says Mrs. Benedikt. "I, too, belong to worthwhile groups. The Holyoke Alumni Association, the Fairfield Debutante Committee. But let me say that while I am here, in this hall, with this splendid cause, my first and only loyalty is for CONTROL."

97

Polite applause. Myra slumps in her seat. It doesn't pay to volunteer information. Better to sit and relax. The members stare at her as if she's a traitor. But after all, there *is* an intimate connection. Without SANITY, there'd be no more people; without CONTROL, there'd be too many people; without CONSERVE, there'd be no room for all those people; without KOOLIE, there'd . . . Pay attention! Mrs. Benedikt is announcing the committees.

". . . and last," looking sternly at Myra, "the Contrillion Coat Checking Committee will be headed by our own Myra Russell."

Politics! Her Decoration job went to someone else. But she mustn't fret. A responsibility is sacred. If only Rose were responsible and dusted. If only Debbie were responsible and let Alex see a doctor. If only Paul were responsible and paid back the loan. If other people were as responsible and old-fashioned as she is, the world would be a worthwhile place to live in. Though, no doubt, a great deal duller.

But no more blue thoughts for today. She must keep her nose to the organizational grindstone. She must shun those tranquilizers, stimulants, barbiturates. Dear Satan, no more pills!

"Meeting adjourned."

❧

"The illiterate black masses of Africa are about to invade the koolie's last home, the Mombazi Game Preserve. And so this proud creature, which has taken billions of years to evolve, can vanish in a single, vengeful safari. Who knows, had our group been on hand, we might have succeeded with earlier species. Roaming across our fenced-in prairies would now be packs of saber-toothed tigers. In the air above, flocks of whip-tailed pterodactyls. In the waters below, swamp-loving carnivorous dinosaurs."

Vigorous applause. A most singular presentation. CONTROL is for preserving people, CONSERVE for saving trees, and KOOLIE is for the birds. To each his own. If every cause didn't have its specialty, they'd be nothing but chatterbox get-togethers. It's the specializing which makes them worthwhile. And if they weren't worthwhile, then they'd be a waste of time. And if you waste time, you might as well be dead. Which is exactly what's going to happen to the human race if something isn't done about it.

Ladies and gentlemen. (It's Mrs. Russell, the well-built woman in the front row who's always quiet as a mouse. Listen, she's about to speak her mind!) *I would like to announce that my son, Paul, has just acquired the Last Forest. Snatched it right from under the nose of the Parkland Commissioner. You may wonder if Paul is greedy, are his only interests mortgages and money? The answer is no. Mr. Paul Russell has decided to postpone my loan which he is unable to repay at the moment because of heavy commitments. Instead, he intends to donate a marsh, which he can't use anyhow, for the propagation of the last remaining koolie birds. Now what do you think of that?*

"Mrs. Russell, wake up! They're passing the basket."

A collection plate in the form of a straw nest. Myra opens her lethargic purse. The dread sleeping sickness. While doing research in Africa. But it's not darkest Africa, it's a dreary meeting hall. And it's not research, it's those pills. And the pills are having an effect on her run-down heart.

99

And her heart is affecting her health, her sight, yes, her very sanity! Either she pulls herself together right this minute or she'll be as marked for doom as the flightless koolie.

～

Midnight at the King's Castle. The tables are packed, the chips are down; men and women focusing their insoluble troubles on a geometric board.

"Quite a surprise," notes Myra, making the first move, an opening. "I mean the Tyranny Bomb announcement."

"They're trying us out," says Igor, making the perfect response. "To see how we'll react. And there's the reaction." He points to his hunched-up customers, like members of a secret sect, praying over their prayer-rug chessboards for wisdom. "And look out the window at the tourists, laughing, drinking, yelling, as if they're any safer than those birds you're always complaining about."

"But sometimes," says Myra, her trap fanning out, "optimism is useful. Do nothing but dwell on disaster, and you'll go out of your mind."

"I've been working on it," says Kovski. "The peace puzzle. Look at it this way: if we can't depend on man to solve his problems, who can we depend on? Sure, we know that somewhere in outer space there must be intelligent life. Far more intelligent than on this God-forsaken planet. But we can never reach them, it's a proven, scientific fact. Why, the nearest star is four light years away. And each light year is six trillion miles."

"What a lot of time. I mean distance," jockeying her knights into battle position.

"Homo sapiens," says Kovski grimly, "is a prisoner within his own solar system."

"How unfortunate," mutters Myra, as she plans a hasty retreat.

"You might say I'm a neo-evolutionist," he shrugs, luring her queen. "But in my opinion, the species' brain is far too complex. That's man's weak link, the organ which will spell his doom."

"Like the poor koolie bird's floppy wings," she sighs, wondering what ever happened to her defense. "Speaking of problems, I've got one myself," trying to forget the world for a change and concentrate on her own impending disaster. "With a brain like yours, I'm sure you could solve it. Supposing, Mr. Kovski, you had a secret bequest and you only had time enough for a few departing words to tell your wife where it . . ."

"Marriage, nonsense. Strictly bourgeois."

"Well then, your mistress. Only three precious words to tell her where you'd hidden your life's savings. And the first word was I or my or buy, something like that. And the second was treasure, seizure, fissure or measure. What would your third word be? You see," she groans, "I'm in a complete stalemate."

"The perfect stalemate," he advises, noting her address in his date book, "is a socio-economic myth." His wiry fingers scoop up her rook. "Too many irresponsible nations. The balance is too tenuous. I'd say the situation is hopeless."

"Maybe not," says Myra.

"Checkmate!" says Kovski.

Myra pulls out a blank check. "Let's see, that's . . ."

"Make it an even thirty cents."

"But Igor, you gave me a whole lesson."

"Thirty cents," he insists. "There are no lessons to be learned. None whatsoever. The only thing left is escape."

"But where?"

Igor scowls. "I'm working on it, Mrs. Russell. Night and day."

If only it were possible. Escape. She gazes out the window at the hordes of weary tourists, desperately searching for pleasure. Sadly, she wanders toward the latched door, toward the outside world, toward the bleak and escape-proof universe.

❧

"The Tyranny Tests must be stopped!" cries Tannenbaum.

"Bravo!" cries Myra.

"A counter plan!" demands Kovski.

"Second the motion!" she demands.

"A petition!" pleads Vic.

"With teeth in it!" an angry plea.

"Action!" shouts Tannenbaum.

"Absolutely!" shouts Myra.

"Meeting adjourned!" declares Vic. "Cinema people, remain seated."

That's what makes SANITY so enjoyable, the way they take off their kid gloves and fight. Because that's what democracy is, that's what evolution is, a struggle. Who knows, maybe for a change she'll be on the winning side.

The projector begins to glow with inspiration. *Hiroshima!* In full-hued rainbow-vision. Blood and thunder, love and disaster, not a single solitary lull.

"A gruesome documentary."

"A masterpiece of gore."

"Never a dull moment," says Myra, awarding three stars. Unanimous. To be shown to the full membership.

The projectionist threads the next film: *Horrors of Hate, Part II. Uncut Version.*

"Wonder what that little bugger will dream up next?"

"You'd think he'd exhausted all the possibilities in Part I."

"A ten-year-old genius. We should get him to join."

"The minimum age is eighteen," says Myra, looking as if she's just made the grade.

The houselights dim. The projector flickers. The committee sits back, ready to judge.

Horrors. The wrong film! She should stop it. Now, before they say something. But no one is saying. They're hypnotized by hate. Of course immorality is hateful, but there are ways of proving a point and ways of glamorizing. And this is glamorization. Demeaning. Frightful. Two men and one woman. Stark, roaring naked. The sound track is unbearable. The poses are revolting. A party film, pure and simple.

Look at those upright members of the Cinema Committee. Not a word of protest. Not even a whisper. Naturally you can find fascination, if you boil everything down to sex. Only Myra boils over with indignation.

But why be a spoil sport? They have a right to be interested as much as she does. And if their interests happen to lie in smut and scandal, that's their democratic privilege.

As for herself, all she wants is to tiptoe from the room. Sex is obviously not her dish of tea. She adjusts her henna hair. Let's face it, she's way past the point of attraction, like a magnet that's lost its grip.

She has got to begin that diet. She has got to shake off pills. She has got to discover new friends. She has got to become involved so deeply, that life will become a splendid baptismal immersion, making her young again, desirable, attractive, charming . . .

The film snaps.

❧

She's been to the smartest movies, sharpened her wits with the latest novels, purged her blues with the snappiest laugh-riot shows. But it's still the same fretful her.

A scientific mudpack. A fashionable hairwave. A colorful zebra furpiece. But it's still the same old her.

She's buried her psyche in Divine Technology. She's penetrated the Serf Defense. She's researched the history of the dying swan for KOOLIE. A compelling lecture to CONSERVE. A donation to COMCHEST. A dollar for the Negro. A dime for the blind. A thousand urgent and worthwhile interests: diagnosing with Dr. Ackerman; picketing with Tannenbaum; gaming with Kovski. Aiding, comforting, cheering. SANITY, CONTROL, CHEMBAN. She's got to pull herself together, keep busy, keep happy, keep trying. Mrs. Russell, her dress rumpled, her zebra trailing on the floor, her curls undone, her eyes worn out, falls asleep in the lonely movie house, having seen for the fourth and last time a movie about love, passion, desire. A movie about despair.

❦

"Your wife looks positively depressed," Myra whispers pointing toward the tiny hayloft.

"I guess they're going to tear down our stables," mutters Paul. "You know how sentimental Syb is."

"But they can't!" declares Myra. "It's not just charming, it's historical."

"They promised to stick up a memorial plaque. Kind of as a reminder. Not every builder is a villain, Mom. Think of it, right over our heads there'll be hundreds and hundreds of families."

"But the fascination will all be gone. Greenwich Village will be just another Bronx."

"Sure," says Paul. "But that's progress. And progress . . ."

"I know," says Myra, staring at her face in the antique mirror, "we've got to accept it. It's just that this house was Sybil's only outlet."

"Now she can concentrate on business instead of butter churns."

"But they're museum pieces. She'll have nothing to do in her spare moments." For the first time, Myra truly sympathizes with her unfortunate daughter-in-law.

Sybil descends the winding stairs. "Damn. It makes you feel so helpless."

"Hold everything!" Myra exclaims. "I've got an idea. Why don't we resist? Form an organization. Take our fight to City Hall," her eyes aglow, her heart inflamed. "An ancient community, an entire street of fascinating homes about to be demolished. A last stand, last-minute committee: STABLES. 'Turn the Tables—Save our Stables!' Pickets. Petitions. Strike," she cries, "strike, strike, strike!"

Myra collapses into a Shaker settee, her brain reeling from pills, from overwork, from worrying about insecticides, Tyranny Tests, population booms, koolie . . .

"Get a hold of yourself," demands Paul. "It's all right to be club happy, Mom. But this is a business, not a hobby. Your organizations are getting you down. You need a vacation."

"On my money? Paul, I . . ." She'd like to give him a patient hint. But if she keeps quiet and seems undisturbed, maybe, out of sheer guilt complexes, he'll repay her. At least half, a quarter, she'll settle for an eighth.

"I'll make all the arrangements. A business expense, courtesy of Happiness Homes. We'll deduct it from the loan."

"How can I go on a vacation?" she sighs. "What about my committees? Cinema, Coat Checking, the Atomic Energy Drive . . ."

"Forget them. Have fun for a change. All expenses paid. While you're away, I'll get over to your apartment and see about some repairs. To hear Rose tell it, you got loose floorboards, holes in the walls, and the ceilings are ready to come down. What's bugging you, Mom?"

"Nothing," says Myra, protesting weakly. "Only who wants to go traveling alone?"

"Then talk to Debbie. Tell her it's my treat."

"Paul, you're a dear."

"STABLES," whispers Sybil, as he gives her a nervous look. "We could organize, explain, refuse."

"Syb, quit trying to resurrect the past. You'll only make a fool of yourself. Look at Mom. You can't stop the world from going where it's headed any more than she can. A protest like that, considering today's housing shortage, would be a hundred percent impotent."

Sybil gives a dirty stare. Paul turns away. Myra reaches for her hat. "Got to run," she smiles, looking like a worn-out koolie bird finally released from its grim captivity. "A vacation in the country. The perfect prescription. Who knows, maybe it'll do me some good."

❧

So that's where she put those strange new pills, inside her money belt where they wouldn't tempt her. Well, better a prescription than to give in to tension. Not that she shouldn't the way the market is sinking, the way the world is crumbling, the way her luggage is coming apart. And then, the gravest problem of all—the missing treasure.

She's got to think logically. Either Ralphy told someone else the clue or she's completely on the wrong track. If he didn't tell, she's got to hush or she'll only tip someone off. But if he told, then she'll have to question every person in her employ. Not just Rose. What if Kovski unraveled the problem because, during a deadly battle of chess, she tried to lead his mind astray? Myra checks for her currency converter. What if Paul and Sybil found it in their tiny stable? She'll order a well-strung tennis racquet, something with genuine gut. Why, even Debbie, praying for her legacy, might stumble on it through some inexplicable miracle.

Nonsense! The treasure is her very own problem and she's got to solve it herself. Even if it's insoluble. Even if her mind is cracking unler the ferocious strain and her hands are trembling like autumn leaves and she's taken too many pills, three, four, even six! When the prescription's confused and the patient's lost count of her stock, do you multiply or subtract the remainder from the dividend? There's nothing more fascinating than a mathematical riddle to take your mind off impending disaster.

Canadian Provincial Time

Myra Russell and Debbie Hilliard decipher the mosaic greeting: *Bienvenue-CHEZ NOUS.* (*Welcome!*)

"An 'International Retreat'," says Myra, quoting the elaborate brochure.

"A vacation abroad," sighs Debbie. "Why that practically makes us foreigners, even if it is only Canada."

"Now I know how it feels to be a refugee. Not half as bad as they exaggerate. Only I wish it were Rio de Janeiro. Carnivals, sugar loaves. Not that I don't admire Canada.

We even have a chapter here. KOOLIE, I mean. Their problem is reindeer."

They approach the desk clerk. Myra fumbles for her French phrase book. "Voulez-vous nous coucher . . ." He raises an eyebrow. She tries again. "Une chambre pour . . ."

"Your reservations," mutters the clerk, staring at them like a sarcastic Parisian waiter, "they are confirmed already."

"Paul thinks of everything," beams Myra, as Debbie struggles with the bilingual registration card.

"Room 13-D," from the marcelled desk clerk. "A little gem. *Very* little. But a fine view."

Debbie shrugs. "Mustn't be choosy beggars. We know how Paul feels about charity. Now, Alex would have insisted on the best."

"It's not fair to compare husbands with sons," says Myra. "Poor Ralph would have insisted on the de luxe, too."

The clerk hands them a chromium stylus. "Just punch the proper squares, so our activity director can fit you in."

Myra jabs the computer card with her pointed dagger. *Archery*—archaic, but fascinating. *Chess*—she's got to keep up her game. *Literary Discussion*—an absolute must. *Music* —something moody. *Nature Study*—naturally.

Age Group. Of all the nerve! Her needle slips past *Business Address*, hops over *Health*, returns to *Faith*.

"I'm sorry, but it isn't on here," she explains to the desk clerk.

"Not necessary to answer," his accent thickens. "We

112

merely ask so we can drive you to the church of your choice. Many of our most distinguished guests are nonbelievers."

"Of course I believe," says Myra. "Only it's not on your list—Divine Technology." She looks him in the eye. "D.T."

"I suppose you'd have to go to Montreal for that," refusing to show surprise. "A rather long trip for a Sunday morning. How do you say in miles? About fifty-nine."

He's guessed! He's staring at her, sizing her up, his private computer card filled with imaginary punchmarks: retired, old hat, past-her-prime, out-of-date, out-of-sorts. As if she's already sixty, as if she's going to do nothing all day but slump in a rocking chair. Well, she is not; she'll keep busy if it kills her. "Hurry," she admonishes Debbie, whose only punchholes are Bridge and Protestant. "We've got to get a move on. So many activities and only one week to do them in!"

The desk clerk gathers the cards, drops them into the calculator, then waves the ladies on toward the *ascenseur* and their garret *chambre*.

A blond face peers from behind the French door. "Kind of cramped here, isn't it? I'm Sandy Dirk, your schedule director."

"Debbie Hilliard," she rushes forward to take his hand. "And this is my old . . ." a pause, "friend, Mrs. Russell."

"Glad you're here. You'll have a fab time. Loads of lovely people. And if you want to be a loner, that's great, too."

Debbie is still holding on to his hand! "I'd rather be active," declares Myra, turning away. "With all this scenery," she points through the attic window, "it would be utter insanity to sit back and ignore it."

Mr. Dirk tries to withdraw his hand. "Of course these rooftop rooms are a bit small for two. If you decide to change, I'll put in a good word at reception." He squeezes past the bureau to take the only chair. Myra and Debbie perch on their empty, narrow beds.

"The decor is lovely," says Myra, examining the cheap oil near the luggage stand. This far from New York, what can you expect?

"That's a Van Gogh," explains young Dirk. "Self-portrait."

"Of course." Myra rushes on before Debbie can say something foolish. "I learned all about him in a lecture— Disfigurement and Derangement in Modern Art."

"Personally, I think he's too old to be interesting," says Debbie.

"We were talking about the painting, not his personality," snaps Myra.

"I can get you an exchange from Interior Decoration," offers Sandy. "If you'd like, we have a terrific twelve by eighteen Blue Boy."

"Tell me about him," says Debbie.

"Gainsborough," Myra notes. "The portrait of a child."

"I'd say he's more like a strapping teen-ager," says Dirk. "Probably about fifteen."

"Too young," decides Debbie. "Isn't there someone inbetween?"

"Used to have a bigger selection," Dirk brushes back his golden crewcut. "Only some of them disappeared."

"Stolen! From a place like this?"

"You can bet they were insured for plenty," smiles Debbie. "Like my husband. Probably for a lot more than they were worth."

Audio chimes. "Guess I've got to run," says Sandy. "Tea in the lounge, ladies. And literary chitchat in the hemlock grove. Meet our guest of honor, Maxwell Fahnstock. Unless you'd rather relax."

"Relax!" protests Myra. "But we came here for a good time."

"Maxwell Fahnstock," Debbie sighs. "Of course we want to meet him. Literature is my favorite passion."

Sandy Dirk presses behind the gold-buttoned elevator boy and disappears.

"You didn't even punch literature on the Activities Card," says Myra, sharply.

"I wasn't interested, then."

"And I suppose the mere mention of Maxwell Fahnstock's name suddenly gave you this great fascination."

"Everybody's fascinated by Fahnstock, my dear. His *Troubles* has put the fun back into sex."

"I didn't know you'd even read it."

"Now Myra, with Alex so sick how would I have time to read a long book like that? But I make it a point to keep up with the reviews."

"You don't think . . ." Myra wonders how to put it without sounding foolhardy. "I mean, Maxwell Fahnstock couldn't possibly be as risqué in real life as he is in his books?"

"Where there's smoke there's fire," says Debbie, as she skewers her earlobes with a fresh pair of earrings. "Isn't that what we came here for? Excitement, glamor. We might even have time for a little romance."

Myra inspects her shockproof watch. "Fourteen-hundred five," she announces. "That means five minutes after four." She begins to unzipper an elegant, peasant-style frock. "We haven't been here two hours, and we're already meeting Maxwell Fahnstock in an enchanting forest. Goodness knows what we'll be up to by the end of a whole week!"

❧

Piped-in music drifts across the sculpture garden. "Brahms, I believe," says Debbie, admiring the limb of an abstract Adonis.

"Too rococo," says Myra, remembering that lecture on appreciating.

"Then it must be early Stravinsky."

"Not nearly classical enough."

"Obviously not Scarlatti," says Debbie, sitting on a stump.

"Of course, the love duet from *Salome!*" shouts Myra in triumph. "It's just before the big lull in Act V when this gypsy widow is buried with the baritone in a pyramid."

"Stop showing off," mutters Debbie, "or we'll be late for the literary chitchat."

They wander over dwarf bridges, stooping under moon gates, circling about a contented Buddha. Myra examines his smile. Wistful. Because he never married. With a family to worry about, he'd look just as harassed as her. On the other hand, with nothing to do but daydream, even she'd seem happy. Well, seeming mournful, happiness isn't everything.

They pause beside a brook to stare at a pair of thrashing fish. "Siamese fighters," decides Debbie.

"But they're eating each other! Look, the big one's got the little one's tail." Myra kneels like a peacemaker beside the troubled waters.

"A family squabble. Better to let nature take its course."

"You're right," concedes Myra. "I suppose fish need an activity, too," as they trudge on. "If you ask me," looking embarrassed, "I think they were procreating."

"Procreating!" leers Debbie, smoothing her duty-free cashmere sweater. "One's got the other's tail in his mouth, and you think they're . . ."

"I wonder," interrupts Myra, "where our director could be? The blond chap."

"You mean Sandy? Why, he's young enough to be your son," says Debbie, looking evil.

"What a neurotic thing to suggest. Debbie, ever since we arrived here, all you've done is think about sex. Don't forget, you're still a married woman."

"That's true," says Debbie, glumly.

"Did it ever occur to you that Alex could have asked me to keep an eye on you? Just the way Rose is keeping an eye on him."

"Good, old reliable Rose. Thank goodness Alex is well enough to do without those night nurses."

"A splendid arrangement," agrees Myra. "Rose is one-hundred percent dependable, she costs you less than a nurse, and I save a whole week's salary." Besides, this way, Rose isn't forced to linger in the apartment, praying, prying . . .

They meander among the hemlocks. "A thousand miles of wilderness," says Debbie, quoting the brochure.

Myra looks grim. "In a few years, even the wilderness will be just another memory."

Debbie stoops to examine a pregnant ladybug. "Now look who's being nostalgic."

"I only meant," says Myra, "that with the Earth filling up the way it is, the Laurentian Mountains are bound to be developed. If Paul could see all this empty land, he'd go out of his mind."

"I thought you came here to forget current events."

"Absolutely," Myra resolves. "Next to keeping busy, forgetting is life's biggest problem."

"Look!" cries Debbie, stopping in front of a swollen toad. "A frog! Must have just eaten."

"I think it's disappointing," says Myra, "how other animals live, tooth and nail, just like us."

"But you wouldn't call *us* animals!"

"Of course we are," says Myra. "It's evolution. You see, we're all part of the same big family. That's why it's so ridiculous to fight each other."

"But animals have to eat, too. After all, didn't you like that lobster we had for lunch?"

"Loved it," says Myra. "Only I made sure not to eat it till it was thoroughly cooked."

"Sure, by being boiled alive," says Debbie. "And then you pass yourself off as a pacifist."

"Debbie, there are two of them! Don't you see what they've been up to?"

Debbie looks closer. "This time you could be right," she laughs. "All the time we were chattering, Mister and Missus Frog have been having a ball."

"Only a twisted mind would find frog fornication funny!" mutters Myra.

Gingerly, they circle the horrified toads, then continue on their talkative way.

❧

Talk Postponed. La Conférence Est Adjournée.

"Fahnstock is up to his neck in writing, I suppose. That's the problem with art, it's so time-consuming."

"I'm dying to meet him," says Debbie.

"If you're overanxious," Myra powders her nose, "it never happens."

"That's what I say about Alex. If I think about it too much, it simply won't come true."

"I imagine you're talking about his recovery."

"Naturally. I'd give anything to help Alex along."

"How wonderful to have a husband again," says Myra. "I mean to see Alex back on his feet."

"Alex is incurable." Debbie's stern pronouncement. "I meant I'd give anything to ease his suffering."

Myra gasps. "But that's euthanasia!" A movement she's always frowned on because of the initiation fee.

"Don't act so intellectual."

"It's no crime to be an intellectual," begins Myra. "If you become a widow then . . ."

"What do you mean, *if?*"

"With all this modern medicine nowadays, Alex, my dear, might even outlive you."

"Myra Russell, what a terrible thing to say! It's my duty as a wife to see that he has someone night and day to watch him suffer. Why, it wouldn't be ethical for me to go first."

"I only meant," explains Myra, "at our age, nothing is for sure. Look at Ralph. Woke up the same as usual, shouting for his grapefruit and his Sunday *Times*. And by noon he was dead."

"The humane way," agrees Debbie. "One, two, three and presto! No pain, no nurses, no expenses."

They gaze up at a pair of circling ravens.

"I wonder . . ." Debbie looks thoughtful.

"Yes?"

"If you sold the rest of your stock and I happened to mention it to Alex."

"Debbie! You swore the D&K would recover!"

"*I* never said that. Alex did. Personally, I think you should dump them immediately."

"And betray my best friend's dying husband," cries Myra. "Out of the question. It would kill him."

"Of course loyalty has its place. But if you decided to unload now, you could still be a wealthy widow."

"It's too late," says Myra disconsolately. "The railroad is down to 7¼. And by my arithmetic, that's enough to keep me going exactly seven years and three months. Unless," her voice lowers ominously, "unless I come into some unexpected inheritance."

Debbie pauses beside a tree marked *Canadian Maple*. "And just what is that supposed to mean?"

"Well," says Myra, breezily, "sometimes people get guilt complexes on their deathbeds. And, if they've given bad financial advice, they try to make up for it in their last will and testament."

"Myra, stop this insane inheritance talk at once! If you think Alex can afford to reimburse a reckless speculator for choosing a bankrupt stock, you've got another think coming. Why, there wouldn't be enough left to feed a churchmouse. I do not intend to be a Social Security widow and that's final."

"Poverty isn't half so tedious when you can suffer with your best friend," confides Myra. "As I see it, the only way we'll ever manage to stand each other will be as financial equals. Let's face it, we'll probably end up companions for life."

"Don't be morbid," says Debbie, raising her voice to be heard above the passionate string ensemble which fills the dining hall with soulful harmonies.

"I can't make out this menu without my pocket dictionary."

"Isn't that violinist charming?"

"Charming and refreshing," says Myra, "to have new scenery for a change." They admire the well-manicured tundra, gleaming through the picture window.

"Look!" cries Debbie. "A pair of doves. I didn't know it

was mating season. Unless they just do it whenever they feel like it."

"That's hedonism," explains Myra, "an old-fashioned philosophy."

"Love by any name," Debbie stares at the violinist, "is still sweet."

"It's nothing but a habit. A trick to make you have too many children. Fortunately, Ralph and I managed to avoid that pitfall."

"The rhythm method?" Debbie frowns.

"Oh no, that's out of style. I merely insisted that sex have its proper time and place. Only when I was in the mood. Which meant when I was in a lull I couldn't break out of. Frankly, I usually preferred to curl up with an interesting magazine. It's much less complicated."

"Lucky you," says Debbie, sipping her Canadian champagne. "Alex is so oversexed, it's pathological. Either I give in to his whims or he'll find someone else."

"They're finished," observes Myra, as the lovebirds fly away. "And you know what? They're just as bored as before. The trouble with sex is, it doesn't work. All that effort for so little pleasure."

"You simply haven't found the right partner," advises Debbie. "You've got to be compatible."

"Ralph and I were *too* compatible." Myra digs into her frog's leg casserole. "I always let him have his own way. Except when I decided to cancel his Sunday *Times*. You see, he'd been reading it so many years, I thought a change would do him good."

"That's what I told Alex. 'Give your blood pressure a

vacation. With homely Rose O'Connor, you'll have absolutely no problem.' Alex was so angry, he wouldn't even wave good-bye."

"Don't encourage a bad temper," warns Myra. "I think that's what drove my husband into his grave."

"What a relief not to hear Alex nagging because I threw out his stock reports or fired some nightnurse cutie," says Debbie. "With Alex and his emergencies, I never have a dull moment to myself."

"I thought I'd be able to relax here," says Myra. "Take it easy for once, drop my responsibilities. But now, I can't help worrying. How are things back in the city? CHEM-BAN, I mean, CONTROL, SANITY. I wonder what they've decided about the Peace March?"

"Let's change clothes," suggests Debbie. "Something informal for the chitchat."

"How about toreadors?"

"Olé!" cry the two women as, arm in arm, they parade down the aisle of potted palms.

∼⌒

Myra frowns at her watch. How is it possible to have a lull in the middle of a glamorous vacation? With every minute so expensive, she has got to find herself an outlet, revive a flagging interest, discover a brand-new pastime.

She peers into the upholstered gameroom, where Debbie the cardshark, is stymied at one club. She'd play bridge herself, but once you've mastered the Serf Defense, Goren seems so boring.

Of course, the library! She's always longed to be a scholar, surrounded by a stack of well-bound volumes, locked in an ivory tower, nothing to do all day but concentrate on one fascinating topic after another.

"A good book," she demands. "Something factual, down-to-earth and specialized."

"And what is *Madame's* specialty?"

"I haven't decided yet," shrugs Myra, leaning against the card catalogue. "Unless . . . But why not, economics!"

"How very interesting."

"The biggest problem," she continues, "of them all."

"As you can see, we've quite a distinguished collection. With guests of our caliber, we must maintain a diverse assortment."

"Nothing like diversification," agrees Myra, rummaging through *Deficit Financiery*. "Never mind economics, I'll tackle something more relaxing. Let's face it, this is a vacation."

"Perhaps you'd prefer the English section," suggests the clerk, steering her away from what are obviously salacious French novels. Translation takes too long when there's only a single week and one has to make the most of it.

"Interesting people should break through the language barrier." Myra catches a glimpse of *Vive La Veuve*. "Besides, I brought my dictionary." She knew it. *Veuve* means her, a widow!

"I suppose you already have *Troubles*?" says the clerk, pointing to the display of Fahnstock's latest.

"I ought to have one for the chitchat. You see, I left my personal copy home. In the States. Manhattan. And could you possibly let me have an extra for my friend, Debbie Hilliard?"

"Take your time, select what you want. There's no rush."

Myra, trying not to rush, emerges with an armful. A pair of *Troubles, War and Peace, Radioactivity for the Layman.* "I prefer important books," as the librarian wraps them. "That's why I avoid short ones. If you've nothing to say, why bother saying it? Unless what you're saying is absolutely vital. Vital means living. And if you're not living, you're . . ." The clerk peers through his bifocals. "Where do I sign for my library card," she concludes.

"We at *Chez Nous*," looking stern, "feel that ownership of books is an integral part of being well-rounded."

"Of course it is. What could be more urgent than the written word—the greatest treasure of them all."

"Thirty-one dollars and thirty cents," says the clerk, firmly, "You can pay at the registration desk."

"But I don't understand!" Myra grabs her shredded handbag. "This is a *librairie*, isn't it?"

The clerk explains. "In French, my dear lady, *librairie* means what you call a 'bookstore.' I regret that we have no *bibliothèque* at *Chez Nous*."

"But you see, sir, *monsieur* . . ." A frantic whisper: "I'm without. Means, I mean. My son is paying for this. You see, I'm a *veuve*."

"Please don't be depressed." The clerk ushers her toward the cash register. "I'm a widower, myself. The main thing is not to feel sorry."

"I agree," says Myra, struggling to be rational. "And to keep busy and to keep your chins up and . . ." He vanishes behind a wall of books. What a plain man. Homelier, even, than Ralph. And that's going some.

Literature, looking ruefully at her thirty-one dollar collection, is definitely not the answer. Not when you're fifty-nine and you're about to meet the author of a $10.95 best-selling Canadian novel and your budget doesn't permit you to increase your cultural status and . . . No, she's got to forget, to enjoy, to endure, to hurry, hurry, the Fahnstock Literary Chitchat!

Myra and Debbie race toward the best seats as Maxwell Fahnstock, his chest puffed like a capon, struts down the stage. Five o'clock shadow. The one thing she won't tolerate. Too much like her late husband and his black-feathered chest.

The author examines his captive audience. Probably lost in a Utopian dreamworld. That's the problem with artists, they're too idealistic. Which, let's face it, is half their charm.

Fahnstock clears his clogged throat. The literati lean forward. "Ladies and gentlemen," he begins. "A show of hands. Has everyone brought a copy to be autographed?"

A few forgetful matrons sneak out the back exit as Myra surrenders both volumes. The great man, with a noble flourish, applies his ballpoint signature.

"How quickly he writes," whispers Debbie. "Wish I had his ability."

"A fat new novel every year," Myra whispers back. "It's a literary scandal. And all in longhand. They say he despises machinery, especially typewriters. I suppose he's never even heard of Divine Technology."

"Forget the theology," says Debbie. "When's he going to get on with the chitchat?"

The audience grows restless. Fahnstock, hand on chin, angrily paces up and down. Trying to think of something fascinating. Suddenly he stops, adjusts his cravat, and gazes longingly toward the ceiling. Second follows second. An excruciating lull! Myra grips her seat. Six hundred miles from civilization and no way to break it.

"By my count, there are still two present who have not given me their *Troubles*," declares Fahnstock. "I signed thirty-eight books, and there are forty people sitting in front of me."

"Good thing we didn't try to get away with it," whispers Debbie, as two sharp-nosed ladies disappear down the aisle.

"Now that we have one hundred percent," he nods, "let's get down to business." The women look spellbound. "Hands," he demands. "How many of you have actually read my latest book?"

Thirty-seven faces turn toward the parquet floor. Sandy Dirk hastily scribbles in his pad. An arm, pudgy and wavering, then proud and resolute—Myra's.

"Great!" screams Fahnstock, stamping on the platform. "A resort for the international élite, and only one person has had the courage and the ambition to face up to *Troubles*. One courageous reader, one enlightened soul." The audience bursts into a spontaneous applause. Myra beams.

"Young lady," says Fahnstock, as she tries to look the part, "kindly join me on the platform."

"Showoff," hisses Debbie.

Fahnstock leads her to a love seat near the silver tea service. "One reader," moans Maxwell. "That's why authors die before their time. Because we despair of finding our audience." He glares at the unlettered assemblage. "Lemon or cream?"

"B . . . both," mutters Myra.

Fahnstock puts his arms around her shoulders. "Now tell me, dear, what was *Troubles* all about?"

"Why, it was about," a prolonged pause, "war," suggests Myra, sipping the curdled tea.

"Excellent! And what was my stand?"

Myra looks desperately around her. "I . . . I don't exactly know."

"Right! You didn't know. That was my purpose in writing this novel. To let you decide for yourself. An artist should never take a position." Debbie, from the front row, is in stitches. "Is that clear?"

"Yes, Mr. Fahnstock. You see, I only read the . . ."

"Will the young lady please inform the illiterate members of our gathering who refuse to consult the book themselves, why I called it *Troubles*."

"Because . . ." Myra hesitates. A pair of hands grind against her thigh, as if he's trying to coach. A split-second lull. Myra ransacks the contents of her brain. "Because," she continues, "that's our main problem. Humanity's main problem—troubles."

"An interesting concept," says Fahnstock, letting go to roll himself a cigar.

"Stop hogging the show," whispers Debbie. Myra, her nose in the air, beams with self confidence.

"We know there are so many parts my readership adore," his hand rests lightly on her arm, "but, as someone intelligent and personable, what did *you* like best?"

"Why, I suppose the love scenes," says Myra, wondering if she shouldn't make a clean confession, that she's only read the thirty-page condensation. But why embarrass the poor man?

"The love scenes," he repeats, astonished. "The very thing which troubled me most. Just for the sake of those," Fahnstock looks at them bitterly, "who never heard of my book until today, what chapter to your mind contained the most vivid love scene?"

"Chapter fifty-nine!" says Myra, pulling the number from a magic hat.

Fahnstock whispers past her earring. "Tell me your name, dear."

"Miss Myra Russell."

He opens his book. "Miss Russell and I," he announces formally, "will enact the rape scene from chapter fifty-nine, entitled: *Man Does Not Live in Bed Alone*. For those who choose to follow the text, it begins on page seven seventy-three."

"No!" shrieks Myra, pushing Fahnstock away. "Miriam's voice was shrill but gentle. Leave me alone."

"Don't be afraid," commands Fahnstock, grabbing her by the shoulders. "Isn't this why you moved to Greenwich Village?"

"Miriam tried to be diplomatic. I've never slept with a non-Caucasian before," Myra confesses, imagining Fahnstock's five-o'clock shadow a permanent discoloration.

"Shut your trap, warned Rayfield. I don't ever want to hear you call me that."

"But you *are* non-Caucasian," protests Myra. "I may be a liberal, but I still believe in calling a spade a . . ."

Fahnstock's face twitches with rage. "Listen, Baby, hissed Rayfield. No matter how black I am, you ain't got no right to call me a Nigger."

"I didn't mean it," cries Myra.

"Then don't say it," begs Fahnstock. "Remember, I'm from the Islands."

"I've hurt your feelings," says Myra. "I only wanted to face the facts."

"Miriam, honey, forget the labels," coaxes Fahnstock. "You got what I call real appeal, said Rayfield, pulling off his tattered undershirt."

"She made room in her bed," reads Myra, moving over in the love seat. "I told you, I never did this before."

"Rayfield sat gently on the edge of the filthy mattress." Fahnstock squeezes next to her. "That's why you're lucky it's me, he said, ripping off his belt. 'Cause you know something?" His hand caresses her knee. "All them stories you heard about us colored guys is true."

"I never think about a person's race," insists Myra, pushing his hand away.

"You white gals is all alike, accused Rayfield, as his fingers wormed their way under her sweat-stained blouse. Just come a rollin' naked with me between them cool sheets, and I'll show you I'm three times the man any one of your lily-white beaus'll ever be."

"But I'm not infatuated with you!" gasps Myra.

"Rayfield was in no mood for talking," narrates Fahnstock. "When he was loaded for action, he wanted in."

130

"Miriam realized Rayfield couldn't wait," reads Myra, trying to avert her eyes. "And suddenly it dawned on her: she wouldn't be able to go through with it."

"Scares you, don't it? purred Rayfield." Fahnstock gives a dirty laugh.

"Miriam knew what Rayfield was thinking," Myra explains. "But if she gave in now, he'd think she was just another slut. Like those sharecropper gals he'd been sleeping with since he turned thirteen."

Fahnstock flips the page. "Rayfield's method was simple: look at 'em, lie with 'em, and leave 'em. He pulled off his sneakers."

"What if I scare him off by acting too pure, said Miriam to herself."

"Suddenly," Fahnstock gropes madly, "Rayfield threw himself on top of her, tearing off her bright-red hair ribbon, stripping away her last shred of decency, penetrating obscenely with his gigantic . . ."

"Stop!" screams Myra, trying desperately to straighten her dress. "Don't give away the plot," she pleads tearfully. "Make them read it themselves."

"She's right!" says Sandy Dirk, turning red. "C'mon folks, a big round of applause for Mr. Fahnstock's reading."

The audience applauds politely as Myra steps down. "A neurotic display of exhibitionism!" whispers Mrs. Hilliard.

Myra shrugs. Just another war story. She far prefers autobiographies. Anyway, Debbie is jealous, as if everything is a matter of sex and neurosis. A strict Freudian. No interest in society. But you *have* to have interests, whether in love or atomic disaster. Only if there's a choice, disaster is so much more important. Otherwise, with everyone gone, there'd be no one left to make love. Though, and it's practically an axiom, if there were more love, there'd be fewer disasters. But not, definitely not, the kind of love Mr. Fahnstock writes about!

"Questions and answers," interrupts Dirk.

"Sir, how did you get started? I mean in your career." An anonymous voice in the back.

"Glad you asked," says Fahnstock. "Y'see, I was always a sucker for boats. But I swore I'd do it on my own. On my own since I was fourteen." The ladies look awed. "So I took every kind of odd job I could find. Dishwasher, stable boy, merchant marines. Finally, I scraped enough together to buy a modest craft."

"A dory?" asks Myra, remembering her course in Melville.

"A forty-four foot sloop. Daddy helped me out a bit. Mom remarried. Never seen either of them since. Became a writer all on my own."

"That's the way to be," nods Myra. "Master of your own sloop."

"Since fourteen!" affirms Fahnstock.

Since Ralphy passed away. Because grapefruits meant more to him than his own wife. Because he took arguments too personally.

"How many of you ladies," leers Fahnstock from his podium, "have had one good bed-session in the past month? Hands!"

Myra closes her eyes, waiting for the dreadful inquisition

to end. Sandy Dirk stares shame-facedly at the floor. Debbie holds her head up high.

"Y'see," says Fahnstock, "that's what comes of taking life seriously."

"It *is* serious," shouts a German accent from the rear.

"Life is a lot of hogwash!" announces Fahnstock.

"But then we'd have no national purpose," cries a lady in the eighth row.

"The only purpose is to breathe," cries Fahnstock.

"Breathing is the key to health," agrees a faddist. "According to my Yoga expert . . ."

"The only expert is a lover," roars Fahnstock, "at the point of orgasm!"

An audible gasp.

"Mr. Fahnstock," says Debbie, standing up, "could you explain more exactly what made you decide to become a writer. I'm thinking of something similar, myself. Of course, nothing like eleven hundred pages. I'd never find the patience. And certainly not the time."

"When Daddy left me his fortune . . ."

"Stocks?" inquires Myra, searching for a good speculation.

"Pants," says Maxwell. "Blue jeans. Biggest man in the business. Well, I thought, what am I going to do with all this dough? Any damn fool can buy a yacht or a duplex apartment. Hell, I decided, I'll buy fame. So I set up a classy journal, wrote rave reviews of my own books. Under different names, of course. Well, before you could say James Joyce, I became the literary sensation of the year. I did it because that was the only way I could be heard. Y'see, I've got something that's got to be heard because it's so damned important."

"And what is that, dear?" from a grandmother on the aisle.

"Buy my books if you want to know!" shouts Fahnstock. "All twenty of 'em. Each one better than the last. Instead of asking me," he points accusingly at Myra, "why don't you lay out a few lousy bucks and find out for yourself?"

"I laid," says Myra. "I mean, I bought. I'm the only one who read you, remember?"

"Of course, of course," mutters Maxwell. "I didn't mean you personally, I meant readers in general."

"Mr. Fahnstock," from someone in the rear, "aren't your books unnecessarily vulgar?"

"If you find a single four-letter word in *Troubles* that you haven't heard before," guarantees Maxwell Fahnstock, "I'll refund your money and double it."

The ladies giggle. "The grand theme of *Troubles*," concludes the author, "is that they're always with us. Get rid of one trouble, and you got yourself a new one. Living, ladies and gentlemen, is one big trouble!"

Applause. Fahnstock raises his hairy arms in gratitude, then struts into the wings.

A lonely, dedicated man. If Ralph had been like that, she'd have prepared his breakfast any way he wanted. But then she wouldn't have been free. The devil with freedom, the main thing is love.

That's the word, the four-letter word she's never known before! She'll find it in *Troubles*, show him, make him explain. A poke from Debbie. The lecture is over. Fascinating. The most fascinating person she's ever met.

❧

"I hope Rose is keeping a weather eye on him. Alex gets so restless when he's deprived of his night nurses."

Myra pats a final dab of cold cream on her cheek. "Don't you worry about Rose. Absolutely trustworthy. My former husband and I had her for over twenty years."

"What do you mean, 'former'?"

"Ralph's deceased, isn't he?" She begins her astringent lotion. "You can't call a man your husband when he's not there any more."

Debbie climbs into the high, narrow bed. "Of course he's your husband," pulling the feather comforter up to her chin. "You're not divorced from him, are you?"

"We never even considered the possibility."

"Then you're still married. 'Till death do you part.' That means you *both* have to be dead."

Myra commences her manicure. "I never thought of it that way," she admits. "I always thought I was free."

"Don't let that Maxwell or Sandy Dirk give you fancy ideas."

"Not a chance." Myra takes a resolute thrust with her emery board. "Though, let's face it, you can only live once."

"So they say," mutters Debbie, sinking into a stupor without pills, television, without anything!

"I must confess," declares Myra loudly, as Debbie's ears disappear beneath the blanket, "that Fahnstock fellow is an obviously dedicated person. The way Paul is to Sybil. And you are to Alex, and Rose is to her saints. And I'm not, I suppose, to anyone. But then, he should be dedicated. After all, literature is a lot more important than blue jeans."

Debbie rolls over.

"Not to knock another trade," Myra rushes on. "After all, my husband, ex, was in soil. For cement. Imagine making a living out of everyday sand. But there are so many apartments going up, we're simply running out of dirt. Not that Ralph could ever be interested in society or problems. He was strictly business. Except at night, when he'd take off his mask and become positively monstrous. If I was in a lull, he scarcely noticed. But let me get lost in an inspiring autobiography, or a complicated crossword puzzle, and Ralph would suddenly get glandular. I never told anyone this before, but . . ." Debbie's deep breathing fills the tiny bedroom with its sleepy monotone. "Once, he even tried doing it while you and I were having a marvelous phone conversation. I had to put my hand over the mouthpiece and tell him off. When I say no, I mean no! Ralphy, poor man, looked like a whipped puppy so I had to promise him some other time. Maybe tomorrow. Maybe next month."

She climbs into bed. The northern moon glares through the tiny attic window. So cold, so lonely. A long, sleepless lull threatens to engulf her. Shoving away the goosedown comforter, Myra snaps on the bedlight, takes hold of her bookmark and plunges into eleven hundred pages of uncondensed *Troubles*.

❧

"Wet blankets make my job a nightmare," complains Sandy Dirk, as their intertwined arms grip the club.

"How could anyone be a wet blanket at *Chez Nous?*" taking a wearisome stroke.

"Let's try that again. This time slice the ball, not the turf."

Myra whacks at a clump of grass. Golf is definitely not her outlet. "What I mean," she says, "at *Chez Nous,* there are so many ways to take your mind off yourself, you hardly realize you exist. It's enough to exhaust a woman half my age. How do I do it, my friends want to know. Well, frankly, I don't know either."

Dirk angrily fills in the excavation. "Wet blankets, Mrs. Russell, spoil everything. In dancing, they're the ones who break legs. In swimming, they're the ones who get cramps. In bridge, they go broke and then complain."

"I guess you mean Debbie. When she loses at cards, she makes everyone feel it's their fault. Spends her dying husband's last penny, then expects him to leave a handsome dowry. A person of very few interests."

An industrious youngster is busy gathering up the golf balls as she hits them into the nearby thickets. Dirk stares. "That's why we don't make a profit," he mutters. "The local lads raid our driving range, fetch up the balls, and make us pay to get them back. When I catch that little whippersnapper, I'm gonna pull down his pants and give him a spanking he won't forget."

Dirk chases the boy into the bushes. Myra is alone. Debbie must be, too. Only she's probably pining for a secret lover. For empty people, sex is just a psychological substitute. But if you already have a worthy cause, why bother? She stares at the nest of mating caterpillars. Yes, if you're an animal, there's no better way to break a lull than overbreeding. Only she's not an animal and never will be. Not as long as she can hold up a picket sign, drop in on a foreign movie, discuss a difficult novel, protest an unpopular war.

That's her love interest! She's in love with peace, in love with life—a love affair with the whole human race. Myra lifts her head toward the sky as a flock of tireless birds, miles and miles of them, heads southward. She has got to get going. Back to New York. To a land of meetings, museums and urgent luncheons. Let's face it—she gazes about her at the lake, the pines, the purple mountain—when you're a widow and all alone, there's nothing less interesting than beauty.

Peevishly, she tugs at the cart of clumsy golfclubs. But if she leaves now, she'll look like just another wet blanket. What would Fahnstock say? And Debbie, and Paul, and Rose?

Three more days to kill. And not a single way to kill them. Unless . . . yes, why not the arts?

Modern Dance: they bend, twist, grovel; they leap, fall, rise; arms, legs, torsos; seeking, creating, expressing. Exhausted, they fall upon the ant-filled grass.

"Strictly for professionals," groans Myra, trying to catch her breath. She's finally finished reading the whole of *Troubles*. Hour after hour, she's ploughed through the endless pages. Not a single satisfactory love scene. Always an interruption: a hidden soldier, a defiant mother-in-law, a sudden gunshot. In the end, everyone was either neurotic or dead. Not that it wasn't interesting. Fascinating, even. Only she never knew what was going on. And now, with her muscles aching from the dance torture chamber, she feels angry with the world, angry with *Chez Nous*, angry with her only friend.

"You look like a thundercloud," says Debbie. "I'm going to the social hall and stir up a foursome."

"A complete waste of time," snaps Myra.

"So is modern dance a waste of time. So are all those organizations of yours. So are golf and archery and literature. So is making love a waste. So is breathing."

"SANITY is not a waste," cries Myra, wishing she could be there tonight for *The Horrors of Hate, Part III*. "And modern dance is good for the glands. And love . . ."

"And love?" smiles Debbie.

"In my opinion," says Myra, "for mature adults, for married women who have been through it all, love is a thing of the past."

"What about that public display you put on with Maxie?"

"Maxie? Since when do you use a nickname for Canada's foremost writer? If Alex could see you, he'd cut you out of his will like no one's business."

"And if Ralph could see *you*, he'd have one of his fits."

"Only," says Myra sadly, "poor Ralphy can't see. He's gone for good."

"And Alex can't see, either. He's in New York."

The women look at each other, signaling a truce.

"Meet you for lunch," nods Debbie. "If you decide to

join me at bridge, fine. Only please, Myra, try to be somebody else's partner. I'd like to win for a change."

"Don't worry. I'm not interested in winning. Paul decided to increase my spending allowance. I just received an airmail postcard. They want us to stay another whole week. On the house."

"An extra seven days!" gasps Debbie. "Just what I needed." She brushes the ants off her velveteen slacks. "Bye-bye, dear. See you at cocktails." She rushes off toward the hemlock grove.

Myra remains sprawled in the grass. For Debbie, who doesn't know the meaning of a lull, passion is everything. Well, not for her. Not at her stage of life, with her body aching from unrelieved tedium. It's so difficult to be creative when you're . . . 60! The numerals brand themselves onto her troubled brain. The last lap. It's about to begin. She's got to do the things she's always dreamed of. Now or never. Hurry, hurry! She leaps into the air.

"Splendid!" shouts the dance instructor. "Why didn't you do that before?"

"Because I wasn't motivated then," cries Myra. "Because suddenly I'm feeling on top of the world. Because," glancing at her watch, "I've got to run. It's late."

A grim reaper, his imaginary scythe sharpened, his diseased bones rattling, chases her headlong toward the next inescapable activity. Which way? Where to?

Toward the sixtieth lap, that's where. Toward old age, gallstones and global extinction. Hurry, hurry, hurry!

❧

The bow stretches taut. She aims her arrow for the bull's eye, for the heart, the lungs, the brain. The others stand around, idly waiting for Myra Russell, who's pushing sixty, to make herself into a fool.

It's Penny Benedikt she's aiming at: Benedikt, who cunningly edged her out of the Decoration Committee. It's a swashbuckling adventurer she's aiming at: a hunter about to trap the last helpless koolie bird. It's an ambitious scientist she's aiming at: a madman, setting his match to the atomic fuse. It's the Pope she's aiming at: who's vetoed the hopes of an exploding population. It's a slumlord she aims at: a moneybags realtor, about to sack the historic stables.

It's Debbie's husband she's aiming at: Alex, who sank her legacy into a rickety railroad; Alex, who'll shame her if she dares reinvest; Alex, whose recuperation will deprive her of a lifelong companion.

No, it's Ralph she's aiming at! At Ralph, who never loved her. Ralph, who thought only of sand, grapefruits and his Sunday *Times*. At Ralph, who left her treasureless, a D&K widow about to turn that hairpin curve marked *Danger-60!*

The poisoned arrow is suddenly released. That's the way! Out of your system. Drive it right out of your hateful mind.

Perfect! A gorgeous, 100%-perfect bull's eye. Poor Ralphy drops dead.

❧

"Debbie Hilliard, don't tell me you came six hundred miles just to play bridge."

"What else is there to do?"

"That's what I've been wondering. You have a heart mixed in with all those diamonds."

Debbie looks anxiously at her partner. "Let me change that bid. Make it one heart instead of four diamonds."

"That's not allowed," says Myra, pulling up a chair.

"In Canada, the rules are different. Right, girls?" The other players look grim.

"Bridge is too much of a drain on the memory," complains Myra.

Debbie spreads her hand. "I'm dummy," she confesses. "It's a good thing you're here. They don't understand a single word of English," indicating the three vultures, who snap up tricks with death-like precision.

"That's why I'm learning French," says Myra. "So I can get along. It's the biggest problem in life. Except, of course, knowing what to do once you get along. Only if you have friends, all you have to do is converse. Not that conversation is everything. I also believe in being active, in participating, in progressing."

"Down four!" cries Debbie. "Don't you think, Myra, you could find something else to do? I can't gab and play bridge at the same time. I'm no genius, you know." She hands a bundle of Canadian dollars to the unsmiling harpy on her right. "Why don't you try swimming?"

"I'm too heavy," laments Myra. "I'm afraid I'd simply sink."

"Sandy's running a twilight demonstration for beginners. Why don't you see what he's up to?" Debbie's tricky fingers deal out the cards.

"I never realized gambling was such an obsession with you," says Myra, as the bidding begins again.

"It's not the money," sniffs Debbie, forgetting last month

142

when she had to wake Alex from his deathbed to beg for more. "It's the enjoyment that counts." Her face hardens into a ruthless mask.

Myra rises from her rocking chair. They don't even notice. Well, you can't expect friends to provide you with entertainment twenty-four hours a day. She heads for the elevator, determined to be happy, busy; determined not to be depressed. Wait till Sandy sees her bareback peach-and-lavender swimsuit. That should cheer him up!

"Kick those feet! Lift that head!" Dirk barks out the commands like a power-mad drill sergeant.

It's easy enough for Sandy, safe and dry on the pool's edge, strutting about in that abbreviated bikini. But for her, in the frigid water, flapping her legs, thrashing her arms, filling her mouth with chlorine, it's a matter of life or . . .

"Grab hold!" he shouts, thrusting out a bamboo pole. If only he'd jump in, a noble rescue. Sandy Dirk, her personal hero.

Myra hauls herself up the ladder, as he grips her clammy hand. "If every client had your spunk, Mrs. Russell, my job would be a cinch."

Myra's teeth chatter approval. "I do my best," she affirms. "Only sometimes I feel I'll never learn."

"Suppose you run along now," says Sandy, drawing away from her shivering body. "I've got to trot over to the social hall. A new course we're organizing, Creative Anxiety."

"How about a nature walk in the sculpture garden?" begs Myra, picturing the dismal evening hovering over her like a vengeful albatross.

"I'd love to, Mrs. Russell. But we'll have to make it some other time." As a bellboy passes by with rum-filled pine-apples, Sandy flexes his well-oiled physique, "Anyhow, we're not dressed for hiking," says Dirk, admiring his sleek reflection in the pool.

"It's just that I'm about to succumb to a lull," explains Myra. "And when you're in a lull, you're halfway to becoming a wet blanket."

Dirk turns from the bellboy to look her in the eye. "None of that, Mrs. Russell. One wet blanket leads to another. Darn thing spreads like the plague."

Myra plops down on her damp towel. "Sorry, dear, but I guess I'm a wee bit winded." She taps her breast significantly. "My heart."

"What's the trouble with your heart?" he demands, pulling a Japanese beach robe over his tights.

"Just an insignificant murmur. Nothing serious. You can hardly hear it."

"Murmur! Mrs. Russell, you should have notified us. Why didn't you punch the registration card under physical defects?"

"Because," cries Myra, "I'm perfectly fine. I'm as well as any teen-ager," pointing to the trim pageboy handing around the drinks.

"Keep Jerry out of this," says Dirk, angrily. "If the boss discovers I've been giving swimming to a cardiac case, he'll have me sacked!"

"He won't find out," confides Myra. "Not if you'll cooperate."

"What do you mean?"

"How about some midnight tennis? To still the lull."

"No more tennis," he says, firmly. "Not while I'm responsible. It could kill you."

Myra looks petulant. "Then meet me on the archery range after the concert."

"Absolutely not, Mrs. Russell!"

"How about a hand of honeymoon bridge?" she pleads. "And call me Myra."

"Mrs. Russell, you're going to catch pneumonia in that skimpy bathing suit. I insist you march right back to your room and jump into some warm clothes, if I have to carry you there myself!" He grabs her by the elbow. Myra slips on the wet tiles.

"Help!"

Dirk tries to clutch the diving board. Too late. Suddenly they're both in the icy-green pool.

"Save him!" cries the bellboy. "Sandy can't swim!" She looks down at the dark form below, like an octopus, its wounded tentacles flapping desperately. Myra pulls herself on shore. A bamboo pole prods the troubled waters. The bellboy's hands reach from above.

Dirk's blond body is spread out at the edge of the pool. Mrs. Russell takes command. "Artificial respiration," she orders. "I learned it in Civil Defense."

Myra presses her fingers into the small of his back. "F'gosh sakes, hands off!" shrieks the bellboy, pushing her away. "That's the old-fashioned method. The latest is mouth-to-mouth."

The nude body rolls over. The bellboy jumps on top. Adolescent lips bite into Sandy's pallid mouth. Pumping, squeezing. Their torsos twist stiffly, their limbs commingle, their faces press together.

"Revolting!" Myra gives a gasp of horror. "His hair! Why, he's totally bald. Even the eyebrows are fake!" She turns away in disgust. A sandy, crew-cut toupee floats forlornly on the deserted pool; the padded bikini sticks out over the edge; the artificial eyebrows frown in the puddle at her feet. Phoney, that's what. A wet blanket. That Sandy Dirk is nothing but sheerest make-believe. A fairy tale, pure and simple.

❧

Myra is out to discover how Debbie spends every endless afternoon. Which, considering the foliage, is more difficult than Sherlock Holmes. In the Game Room, Mrs. Hilliard snatches the last trick, pockets her winnings, and rises from the table. Her three speechless friends push back their chairs.

Hurry. Myra turns toward the registration desk, down the service stairs, through the rustic kitchen, over the stacks of firewood, behind the imitation totem pole.

Debbie, humming a lumberjack folk tune, strolls into the depths of the forest. A nature hike. Or will it be a brief encounter on a carpet of moss? Myra darts into a bush labeled *Poison Sumac*.

Maxwell Fahnstock! She's grabbing his arm, her fingers like claws, her nose like a parrot's, her eyes like a crocodile's. A pair of mismatched lovebirds— Debbie Hilliard, Manhattan's biggest illiterate, holding hands with Montreal's most prominent author. After all her well-rounded lectures, all of Kovski's brain-stretching chess lessons, who does

146

Fahnstock prefer but a perfect dummy. Someone who's not even a widow, not even available.

The mating of opposites, a literati with a trollop. She's heard of things like that in French novels. But in French Canada? Myra dashes across the pine cones, over the perma-frost, toward the split-log theatre.

"Bonjour," she snaps. "Nice afternoon for a walk."

"You remember Mrs. Russell," says Debbie, bitterly. "She's the one who read your condensation."

"I've ploughed through the whole book," says Myra, indignantly. "All ninety-six chapters."

Another woman. Youngish, with a haughty smile. "My mother," introduces Maxwell, "Viola Cummings."

"Mother!" cries Myra. "You said you haven't seen her since you were fourteen."

"Viola is the third wife of Mom's fourth husband," explains Fahnstock. "That makes her my stepmother, seven times removed. Mother handles all my tour arrangements." He pats Viola's hand tenderly.

"It's been great chatting with you, Myra Russell. Meet you tonight after cocktails," says Debbie, icily.

"Perhaps," notes Viola, "the lady is interested in op-era."

"Myra? Why, she'd be bored stiff."

"Opera, it so happens, is one of my chief pastimes. I'm a regular subscriber at the Met. Odd Thursdays."

"We were working out an original libretto," says Maxwell. "Mrs. Hilliard, here, suggested a brilliant scenario." A vain smile from Debbie. "I'm working on the versification, and my mother, Viola, is adapting melodies from Buxtehude. We're having the first run-through this afternoon."

"I can't believe it!"

"Wanted to surprise you," says Debbie, shyly. "We're not ready for a public performance, yet. Maxwell suggested I join the chorus."

"But that sounds fascinating. Please," looking at Debbie's new-found confidante, "couldn't you let me try out?"

A whispered consultation. Myra catches *spoil everything* from Debbie's purple lips.

"Mrs. Russell, we've decided we can use you," announces Fahnstock.

"When the finale begins," directs Viola, "there's a gorgeous crowd scene. I'll cry 'Amazons,' and you and Mrs. Hilliard will rush on stage, surround the husbands, and execute them."

"I'll fetch a club from the prop room," says Maxwell, heading backstage.

"But what do we do with the bodies?" asks Myra, as they enter the dressing room.

Viola shrugs. "Not finished yet. It's a Work-in-Progress. Just sit down and make yourself comfy. It doesn't happen till the very end."

"Well," says Myra, "I guess you can't be an artist if you don't have patience."

Fahnstock drags in a monstrous caveman's club. "Try this for size," he mutters, rushing off to rehearsal.

"But where are my lines?"

"It's all done with gesture," Debbie explains. "When you

see the husbands, come charging in full of hate, and make your face look horrible. That's called acting. Imagine someone you despise in real life. Then start whacking away with your club so the audience will realize you're furious."

"Frankly, I'm not capable of hate," says Myra. "The only thing I hate is hate itself." She reaches for the mascara. "I'm strictly for peace."

"You must have had an occasional fight with your husband."

"Naturally." Myra takes off her plaid beret. "There were times I couldn't stand him. When he refused to take me to a new hit show, and we had to sit home doing nothing. When he nagged about breakfast, and complained about his paper being late. Why, I could have killed him. But hate him? Never."

"Listen, that's the love scene," says Debbie, as the counter-tenor wail drifts backstage.

"If they're in love, why are they screaming?"

"Because that's the kind of couple they are."

"Like Ralph and me. We screamed, too. Only it was friendly. An outlet."

"Alex never raises his voice. He just burns. You should see him. Turns red as a beet. He'll kill himself that way. But there's nothing I can do. I refuse to be dominated, and that is that."

"Ralph never kept it corked up." Myra smears her face with greasepaint fury. "When he was mad, the whole house shook. No secrets with my husband. My late husband, that is." She streaks her forehead with savage vermilion, as her thoughts turn toward Ralph, shrieking those curious last words—*I treasure*. Certainly not pleasure! So self-centered, he wouldn't trust the bank, his lawyers, his faithful wife. She paints a hateful sneer across her lips. "No," she mutters, "Ralphy never corked it up. When he got mad, it was like a giant thunderstorm. I hated it at the time. But now," choking the air with her talc, "I sort of miss the excitement."

"You should see mine when I give the sack to an eye-catching nurse," chuckles Debbie, cleverly blacking the edge of each tooth, as her mouth fills with venemous fangs. "Alex is like a capped soda bottle, packed with explosive bubbles. It's impossible living with a man like that. He refuses to improve because he's too psychosomatic, and he refuses to get worse because he's too scared of dying. Thank goodness there's no nurse to flirt with now. Let him ogle Rose O'Connor's scrawny legs to his heart's content."

"I think that's what scared away all her men," says Myra. "If Rose's face is plain, at least it's tolerable. But those bowlegs!" She pencils a cruel squint at the corner of each eye.

"Frankly, I'm still worried. What if he talks Rose into taking a day off?"

Myra practices swinging the club. "It doesn't pay to fret," she advises. "That's what killed poor Ralph. Do something a bit out of the ordinary, and he worried himself to pieces. Like grapefruits. He insisted they be trimmed just so. One morning Rose was sloppy and Ralphy had a tantrum. That's when I took over. I marched right into that kitchen, rolled up my sleeves, and decided I'd had enough. Listen, I said to myself, I am not going to spend every breakfast the rest of my life eating grapefruits in the same, dull way. After all, even citrus can be interesting. So I pulled out my old cookbooks and there it was: a recipe for grapefruit pâté, ground into a delicious mash, scalloped, and topped with a curl of garlic. I suppose I should have warned Ralphy, and not just suddenly appeared, smiling as usual, with the pâté under a special glass bell. That was my big mistake. You see, it happened to be the very morning I canceled his Sunday *Times*. Ralph had never missed an issue since the age of eight. But I decided to switch to a less popular paper, so we'd have some conversational tidbits our friends hadn't already read. When I put the tray down and spread out *The Christian Science Monitor*, there was an awful moment of silence. That's when Ralphy had his fit. He was yelling for his grapefruit. He was yelling for his newspaper. He was yelling for Rose to stop yelling. Finally he drove himself into a fatal attack. After whispering some mysterious words, words which I'll always treasure . . ."

"Amazons!" shouts Viola from the wings.

". . . poor Ralph had a stroke and died that afternoon."

"Amazons! Amazons!"

Myra and Debbie charge hatefully onto the boards, hurling their papier-mâché clubs. The husbands go down in a spiteful bloodbath. The desperate singers howl, the music shrieks, the Amazons stage a feverish and horrifying climax.

❧

Nature is out of tune. The Arctic air is attacked by a tropical rainfront. An epidemic of sniffles. The opera, canceled; the golf course, flooded; the Bohemian Fiesta, a fiasco: with Sandy refusing to frug, with Fahnstock guarded by his fake mother, with Debbie frantically chasing both of them like an unemployed geisha.

Myra takes a last fling at bridge—a waste of money. Lessons on the videoharp—a waste of music. Archery—a waste of arrows. Hour follows hour. Slowly, irrevocably, she's turning into a genuine Hudson Bay wet blanket.

She's tried everything. *Self Expression Through Oils.* What if there's no self to express? *Expanding the Ego.* But her ego is already at the breaking point. *Faith for You.* All they discussed was religion. Which, as everyone knows, is completely out of date.

Then that awesome Montreal headline: TYRANNY TESTS THREATENED! And the local newssheet's: C'EST LA GUERRE? As if, by dodging her organizational duties, she's been fiddling around while the globe prepares to burn. A stirring speech by the manager, reassuring the international lullards that it's safe because they're miles from the target. A fervent promise: when the cities vanish, he'll reduce the rates. Reduced rates, poppycock! If they knew her financial condition, they'd abandon her without mercy to the radioactive flames.

And Sandy Dirk, explaining his underground plans: songfests and bingo in the basement shelter. So even the Apocalypse won't be dull.

Myra jumps into her moccasins. She mustn't let it happen! Sixty, in a place where no one cares. She's got to get back to New York, back to her meetings, her vanishing treasure, to life itself.

They shouldn't have stayed the second week. She'd almost forgotten. Her birthday. Maybe she'll keep it to herself. After all, there are such things as secrets. Like Ralph's secret cache. Like the President's secret schemes for total war. Like Alex's secret doubts about D&K. Like Happiness Homes' secret blueprints to develop the planet. Like Sandy Dirk's secret hairpiece, secret smiles, secret highsigns to the bellboys. Like the whole globe, spinning drunkenly toward a grotesque and secret rendezvous with destiny.

"Debbie," she cries, interrupting a grand slam. "Forget your card tricks. I've got to tell you. Rose called me this morning. It's about Alex. She tried to keep it a secret. A relapse. She's hiring a new night nurse."

"F'God's sake!" screams Mrs. Hilliard, as her vulnerable opponents gasp in French.

"A young one," she whispers. "A terribly good-looking red-head."

"C'mon!" Debbie grabs her winnings while the scavengers look on in anger. "There's still time to make the last plane!"

"The last plane," shouts Myra, racing toward the valises, "leaves in half an hour."

"Maybe," cries Debbie, "poor Alex is already dead. Maybe," she cries, "he's pulled me out of his will!"

"The airport!" Myra commands. "If there's a will, there's a way. Hurry, Debbie, hurry! A matter of life or death!"

Twilight Saving Time

Sybil backs out of the kitchen, tiptoeing like an angora goat. Suddenly she wheels around and thrusts out the cake. Three vast layers, one for each stage of life: infancy, adolescence and death. "Happy Birthday!" she roars.

"I thought you'd forgotten," says a discouraged Myra, counting row upon row of burning tombstone-candles. "Fifty-eight," she mutters, "fifty-nine. Sixty! But that's too many!"

"Last year we took your word for it," snickers Sybil. "This time we looked it up."

"Sixty," she repeats. "The last lap. I feel terrible."

"C'mon, Mom. Blow out the candles so we can eat the cake."

"Our last celebration," sighs Sybil.

"She means the last one here. Y'see," explains Paul, "they finally decided to tear down the stables."

"Progress," says Myra, thinking of her vanished year, the fifty-ninth, gone forever. "It's inevitable."

"See, even Mom agrees. Snap out of it, Syb. So we'll move into a new apartment. Something with a modern bathroom and no more stairs to climb."

"You can't stop technology," are Myra's last fifty-ninth words as she commences to extinguish the candles. "Phhh!" She can hear her murmuring heart. "Phhh!" Eight more to go. "Phhh!" Two more. Her heart is pleading with her: out with them, the minutes, the wasted decades.

"Congratulations, Mom! Now let's get at it. And no more sad songs from you. Things are looking up. By God, the way real estate's booming, maybe we'll even take care of you in your old age." Sybil plucks out the candle-years and tosses them into the trash basket. Paul begins to stuff himself with the ghoulish pastry. Myra, sixty if a day, stares vacantly at the early-American pendulum as it swings its relentless way toward oblivion.

～～

"Fellow Technologists, the divine and natural forces of the universe are preparing to carbonize our planet!"

"Alex was no worse than usual. I don't know why we had to leave so soon. Just when I had seven no-trump."

"Debbie, I had a birthday last night."

"It's neither emotion nor belief we need, it's reason. And reason tells us that catastrophe is inevitable!"

"Not that Alex is well. Frankly, I'm expecting the worst."

"Paul threw a party for me. A surprise, a terrible surprise."

"Scientific research proves that we are imprisoned forever inside our solar system. There is no escaping the future. We must be as dispassionate about the ending as we were about the beginning!"

"Debbie, you can't imagine how many candles there were."

"We must not avoid, we must not shun technological developments. We must simply comprehend them!"

"I never pry into the secrets of friends."

"The human body is a simple agglomeration of inanimate atoms, mere electrical forces. If these molecules are destined to be converted into carbon dioxide and dust, then that is Divine Planning. Let us understand this plan, let us welcome this plan, let us participate in this plan. For Armageddon is frightening only to those who fear progress. Amen!"

"Just how old *are* you, Myra Russell?"

Mrs. Russell searches the auditorium's chipped ceiling for Divine Inspiration. She turns to examine Debbie's gray hair, her sagging jowls, her inquisitive face. Then, proudly, Myra tosses two tarnished quarters into the stainless-steel collection plate. "Fifty!" she declares, looking Debbie straight in the eye.

❦

When her hair is completely white, she'll dye herself blond. When her wrinkles become unbearable, she'll take to plastic surgery. When her teeth are all gone, she'll insert synthetic dentures. When she grows weary of hair dyes, surgery, her plastic smile, she'll slip herself an extra tranquilizer.

An end to birthday cakes! Too much like Rose with her high-church candles. No more clock-watching, no more flipping the pages of her restless calendar. She'll be sheltered from time, shielded from anxiety, encased in a perpetual glacial lull. She'll be entombed, like an extinct mammoth, in a block of impregnable ice.

"Mrs. Russell, a person who owes her domestic three weeks' wages got no business thumbing through fancy travel magazines."

"Rose, don't you worry. Something will turn up. Just leave everything to me. I'll find it, even if it means renting one of those mine-detecting machines."

"Mrs. Russell, if you think I can afford to starve while you dream about them phoney contraptions, you can just forget it. 'Cause I can tell you one thing. I want my pay, and I want it now."

"Who knows," nods Myra, sighing at the poor, faithless creature. "Maybe, Rose dear, everything will work out for the best."

❧

"Does CONSERVE accept the money or not?" demands public relations man Victor T. Brown as he lights up a popular brand of cigarette.

"What delicious cookies, Mrs. Russell."

"My maid baked them. Not that *I* don't know how. Only nowadays, who can find time?"

"Blood money!" objects an elder. Myra looks at her with pity. A fossilized remnant of the last century. "Nature took hundreds of millennia to be created," cries the fossil. "Don't let it be destroyed for the sake of a miserable donation."

"Made with cinnamon," confides Myra.

"It's not miserable," cries Vic. "It's ten thousand dollars. If we postpone the battle and get the commissioner off the hook, he's sworn to conserve an entire mountain upstate."

"Indeed," sneers the holdout, as Myra passes her a cookie. "Sure he'll preserve the mountain, long as no one wants it. But watch that promise turn into a lie the moment they invent a way to level mountains."

"Never!" pledges Victor. "Leveling's much too expensive. Besides, it's a six-hour drive from here. It'll be decades before the city's that big."

"Return the check!" demands the troublemaker.

Mrs. Russell, out of cookies and out of sorts, gazes at the lonely rebel. Impoverished and gray. Just how she'll end up if she doesn't find a new lease on life. Naturally she can tint her hair, but underneath, she'll be as white as Sandy was bald. Naturally she'll use rejuvenating lotions, but peel off the veneer and it will still be the same wrinkled her. Of course she can make Paul repay the loan. Trouble is, he'll weasel out of it, the same as usual.

"Ten thousand dollars is nothing to sniff at," continues Vic, pounding the podium. "Happiness Homes doesn't *have* to pay us a red cent."

"I am disgusted," announces Myra. "Here the world is

about to explode into smithereens and you surrender for a measly ten thousand."

"You mean they would have offered more?" cries Vic.

"I mean the purpose of CONSERVE is to fight speculators nail and tooth. Frankly, I ought to demand a refund."

"I don't understand, Mrs. Russell."

"The money I contributed to save the Everett White farmstead. If you're not going to conserve, then be decent enough to return my donation."

"But it's in the general fund," explains Vic Brown. "Some of it for personnel, some of it for pamphlets, some of it for public relations."

"Sure, for *your* firm!" cries the dissenter.

"Madam," explains Victor, patiently. "There is no conflict of interest when we choose a concern which I know can be trusted. Just as there is no reason why Mrs. Russell here shouldn't be an ardent CONSERVationist, even though the chief speculator threatening to tear down the Last Forest is none other than her own son, the president of Happiness Homes!"

Sounds of betrayal. Rumbles of revenge. Myra slips away from the stunned assemblage before they can lynch her, before they can stone her with her own now inedible cookies.

No more getting involved in problems. Better to sit home in a corner, bored to tears, than to be an organizational wet blanket. Far better to wait it out for that golden Judgment Day when Paul, like a sainted son, decides to repay his loan, principal, penalty and compounded interest. A divine and heavenly dream. But meanwhile there's a world to reckon with. And debts. And bills. And a crumbling economy. "Taxi!" she cries. "Hurry, dear, rush me to the Stock Exchange!"

❦

What if the price of gold goes down? Myra clears the mantle of Rose's Hollywood ikons. Then her treasure will be devalued, plummeting to a new low. A hasty search behind Rose's collection of miniature Madonnas.

Who said the treasure is gold? A flipping of pages, Rose's *Single Girls and Sex*. Suppose it's nothing but a bundle of of worthless D&K's? She replaces the chromium crucifix. Then she'll be a worthless widow with a worthless treasure. An ominous creaking.

"Rose, what a surprise!" Myra rushes into the dining room.

"You're supposed to be at the chess parlor, Mrs. Russell. That date book of yours has you down for a lesson."

"Isn't it your day off, dear?" shielding Rose's diary. Which she refuses to read because it's full of make-believe smut. "I have other things on my mind besides checkmates. For instance, my private engagement register is missing, and I thought . . ."

"Meant to tell you," says Rose, slamming the door of her room defiantly, "I had to scrub the cover. Full of dust. Guess I left it in the cupboard."

"Don't you think, dear, you could let me take care of the more personal documents myself?"

"Mrs. Russell, it certainly don't pay to have a conscience. Now I get yelled at for snooping. Anyhow, your personal dates are safe with me. You got that book locked tighter than a treasure chest."

163

Myra takes the engagement book and marches to her bedroom. Kovski is right, these days a balance of powers is an impossibility. She examines the tiny padlock. As if the secret is hidden there in her diary! As if her well-packed timetable contains the answer to Ralph's million-dollar riddle.

Which if solved, would make her wealthy. Which would demonstrate Kovski is wrong, that the balance of power *can* be maintained, if only she'll pay Rose's back salary and once again become mistress in her own household.

Meanwhile, unbalanced and depressed, she must live out the day. She must bury herself in each passing moment, interest her ego in each evaporating second. It's that stage of life when waking up is no more than a nervous possibility. And breathing the next breath is a bare probability. As if it's all a grotesque game of roulette, played on a giant astronomical wheel, with the disordered white Earth spinning round and around until suddenly the fatal number turns up. But best not to be philosophical. Let it take her by surprise. Let death be one more fascinating moment, an unexpected pause in her battle with war mongers, population boosters, koolie haters. A devastating interruption to her struggle against poisoned air, leveled forests, ravaged roadsides.

"We'll march on City Hall!" she shouts to Sybil across the weary telephone. "STABLES will threaten the mayor with votes!" She pictures the outraged pickets storming the Bastille of Municipal Corruption.

"Sure the past is great," mutters Paul on his extension. "Only listen, Mom, a hundred house-hungry families could live on top of our little stables."

"We'll organize a protest!" Myra goes on. "Enough of this dialectic."

"Mom, I may as well spill the beans," confesses her profligate son. "When these stables are out of the way, Happiness Homes is going to replace them with the most luxurious Maisonette in all of New York."

"You're kidding!" gasps Sybil on her wooden receiver.

"The D'Agostino Arms," says Paul. "In memory of Mr. D'Agostino's mother who died in a sixth-floor walkup tenement."

"A shame," says Myra, looking out the window in the direction of City Hall, now hiding in a haze of deceit.

"You mean I can head the renting office!" exclaims Sybil. "But Paul, doll, why didn't you tell me?"

"I've got to run," cries Myra. She hangs up angrily. Strictly a lost cause. When your own son betrays you, what can an idealist like her say?

She stares out into the thickening air, at the littered sidewalks twelve stories below, where Myra Russell, a ghostly apparition, is vacantly handing out imaginary pamphlets. Something about beautifying the city, something old-fashioned about preserving historic sites, something visionary about a cleaner atmosphere, more parks, fewer cars. Something about an improved, a happier, a more fascinating place to live. Myra's eyes spurt chemical tears as the yellow fumes —radioactive haze from Nevada, technological droppings from Tahiti, cobalt from the Sahara—as the smog, filled with an odor of decaying flowers, silently closes in on her.

❧

165

"But Alex is knocking on death's door," whispers Debbie. "It's out of the question."

"I have to see him. A matter of life or bankruptcy."

"Please Myra, don't dramatize. My husband is sinking away in that very room. How do you think I feel?"

"Then goodbye!"

"Now don't go away mad. Of course I'll slip him your message. Only for goodness' sake, don't talk so loud."

"The railroad," she cries, "it's down to 6½. Ask him if it's going back up or should I call it quits?"

The funereal gates swing open. Myra peeks into the room. Filled with engines and wires, transfusions and cathodes. A grizzly experiment, the prolongation of inhuman life.

Debbie emerges. "The way the world's going, he says there'll either be a boom or a bust."

"Which one?" pleads Myra. "Ask him which!"

If she doesn't discover a miracle, yes, one of Rose's papal miracles, she'll be broke before she realizes. 6½. Just enough to survive for six years, six months. Then, as Kovski says, war might be the only way out. A catastrophic and final solution to her heartrending and insoluble dilemma.

Debbie re-emerges. "Nobody knows," she whispers.

"But the D&K!"

"Myra Russell, a man who happens to be my husband is passing away right from under our noses. And you have the gall to ask him how to make more profits. If that isn't selfish, I don't know what is."

"I suppose you're right," sighs Myra. "Anyhow, why sell when it's worthless? I'll simply have to have faith." Faith, the straw that broke the camel's back. The camel that was Ralph, faithfully bearing his treasure across the sands of time, the sands now trickling toward the clock's bell bottom.

"It's not as if you don't have a son to fall back on," interrupts Debbie. Myra nods glumly. "All I've got is Alex. And Alex, my only hope in this world, refuses to discuss his will. I wouldn't be so annoyed, except he doesn't have a dime of insurance. My hubby believes exclusively in stocks."

"Which one?" begs Myra.

"D&K, I imagine. Unless he has something up his sleeve. With Alex, you can never tell. That's why I'm so busy, night and day, trying to get his affairs in order. After all, my dear, a widow without money is like a yacht without a sail."

Myra clutches her canvas handbag. "I couldn't agree more," she says bitterly, thinking of her yachtless, austerity budget. Which she must simply refuse to expand. With inflation just around the corner, it's her duty to do without.

She refuses to mend her color TV, now drenched in mournful purple. She refuses to repair her ailing watch, now busy losing ten minutes a day. She refuses to replace her Apostle dinner dishes, now down to one. She refuses to sell her D&K, now down to 6. She refuses to raise Rose's salary, now eight weeks overdue. She refuses to lose herself in travels, mansions, her subscription dreams, now all expired. She'll sit immersed in a permanent lull. Which is the same as committing suicide. Which is exactly the same as death. Which, even if it is progress and inevitable, she refuses to accept.

No! She'll do the necessary. She'll buy herself a split-second timepiece, pay off Rose, mend her color-blind television, subscribe to cut-rate, lifelong renewals. If death is nothing but an eternal, agonized lull, then she has got to go on mending, renewing, fighting for the right, yes, the Divine and Democratic Right, to be fascinated.

❧

"How long," asks Myra, "will it go on murmuring?"

The doctor reviews his solemn charts. Like Paul's microscopic subdivisions, the human anatomy parceled into pipeline nerves, foundation bones, boulevard arteries. "The body, Mrs. Russell, is as complicated as power politics. One never knows. You could have years and years. Or an explosion next month."

"Isn't that Bomb business terrible," agrees Myra, trying to shield her mind from her troubles. *Troubles.* Fahnstock certainly put his finger on what's wrong with the world. Oh, for a pastoral Garden of Eden, a face immune to wrinkles, a planet immune from disaster. "Will the treatment be very . . . expensive?"

"It all depends on one's means."

"Nothing, Doctor Ackerman, simply nothing! Not if I go on living. My stocks are down to $5\frac{1}{2}$."

"Then why not sell while the going's good?"

"Because the going isn't good. It's at rock bottom. I've got to wait till the railroad gets on its feet again. A merger. A subsidy."

"Meanwhile, I suppose I'm the one who has to suffer."

"I won't hear of it," says Myra, generously. "Whatever your fee, I expect to pay. I've always been against subsidized medicine. Except, of course, for the indigent."

"Of course," says Ackerman, indignantly.

"I must know," she insists, staring into his vacant spectacles. "So I can plan my expenses. Be frank, is it a few months or a few years?"

"It could be only a few days," says the doctor, calmly puffing his cancerous pipe. "Or . . ."

"But that's no time at all!" she interrupts, trying not to fall into the trap, Dr. Ackerman's little ruse. Like the Serf Defense, which is no defense at all. Take a young doctor, bored by good health and longevity. Add a gullible patient, with an imaginary ill, an exaggerated murmur. Multiply by a thousand minor aches and useless pains. And so, to escape his daily lull, the physician mistakenly stretches a point.

"I'm no astrologer, Mrs. Russell. Just a simple doctor, a human being."

"Aren't we all," she shrugs. "Anyhow, I never said you weren't. It's Debbie said you're inhuman, charging what you do. But couldn't you just re-examine those X-rays? If I only have a few years to spend, tell me so I can spend them profitably."

Dr. Ackerman holds them to the light. "Mrs. Russell, you'll live longer if you forget your heart ailment and think of something else. Diversions, friends, there's no cure like enjoyment. Yes, offhand," scanning the ghostly negatives, "I'd say the prognosis is guarded."

"Thank you, dear," as she rushes madly toward the asphalt city, a thousand perilous thoughts pressing on her mind, "that's just what I wanted to know. The truth."

❦

"And now," Kovski steps up to the velvet-draped mound, "the official unveiling of our Neuron XIX. Ours for a whole month. A full-time computer's much too expensive for a small outfit like SANITY."

"Small, but growing," adds Victor.

He's certainly an idealist. Never without his smile.

"So we rented the Neuron on a short-term lease," continues the Chessmaster. "If we can't solve the peace puzzle by Independence Day, it'll be too late."

"Don't worry," smiles Vic. "If our petition doesn't work, we'll think of another gimmick. The main thing is hope."

"Hope isn't enough for me," cries Sid.

A realist. Always with a frown.

"Tannenbaum, you're out of order," shouts Brown.

A homely busybody in the tenth row rises to speak. Why are SANITY women so plain? And CONTROL ladies so prim, and KOOLIE women so flighty? Must be psychological, reflects Myra. Look at her, a member of them all. Prim, just comfortably; flighty, to a fault; plain . . . not at all! Not after her latest mudpack, sauna, tummy massage. And, to cap it off, that new hairpiece, a streak of silver amidst her billowing, brunette clouds.

"Mrs. Russell did yeoman's work in selling raffles for our Neuron XIX," grins Vic. "And Maisonette, that swell realty outfit, generously offered us a basement office."

An illegal tax deduction. She heard Paul whispering to his bedroomette wife. It's because of them that the stables are condemned, that farmer White is living in a fake Colonial. And, as if she doesn't have enough troubles: Alex, insisting he can't give a speculative tip because his lips won't move any more; Rose, insisting on her back pay because she's supporting an imaginary lover; Debbie, insisting on faith. How can you have faith when the world around you is about to die? When you yourself are dying every minute.

Action! The Bombastics must outvote, outshout the Beggars. Tannenbaum is right, poor boy. Separated from his alimonied wife. Trying to make peace not only with her, but with the whole wretched universe. A clear case of emotional compensation.

Myra, staring blankly at the SANITY book collection, works on her sparetime problem. *Lie—treasure. July—treasure.* But of course! *July,* the page where he hid the clue; *July,* the month of the Tyranny Test. She must rush to her library, thumb through the engagement books, tear off the covers, rip open the bindings, crack the code, pace off the distances. But meanwhile, there's the world to attend to, the world with its flickering heart.

"Computers are all very fine," says Tannenbaum, "but we need more than mere knowledge. I mean a march, a demonstration by all the peoples of all the world."

"A terrible image," groans Brown. "Think of the public."

"That's just who he is thinking of," cries Myra, applying her lipstick. "The public, about to perish because of our indifference. The public, about to be cremated because all we do is petition. I agree with Kovski, we must have knowledge. But I also agree with Tannenbaum. Either we act or we'll be nothing but baked bones."

"A peace parade," demands Tannenbaum.

"A new petition," insists Victor.

"Both absurd," notes Kovski. "Why raise questions if you don't have the answers? The only goal now, my friends, is to save our own skins."

"That's what they said at Buchenwald!" counters Tannenbaum. "But saving one more skin isn't enough. Look at all the fuss the newspapers are making about the Cave Girl. Why, we wouldn't have the slightest hesitation to destroy humanity." He shuffles his notes. "And yet we cringe before the spectacle of a nine-year-old kid missing in some cave. It breaks our poor stars-and-stripes hearts. That's why our enemies say we're nothing but a nation of soap opera fiends. A nation of evil sentimentalists. A nation of slick slogans and hopped-up headlines. Well, headlines aren't the same as reality. Because reality today means extinction. Not just the extinction of a nine-year-old girl, but the extinction of us all. Of fathers, mothers, children. The annihilation of grandparents, of embryos, of animals, of trees. The annihilation of the planet. The annihilation of the future. And all we can do is fantasize about a little lost girl. But it's *everyone's* life that's in danger." Myra looks around nervously. "It's *you* who are about to be turned into what my colleague so aptly termed 'baked bones'." She grips her seat. "It's *your* body that's about to become flaming flesh, intestinal rubbish, poisoned dust!"

A round of applause. A powerful speaker. A fascinating evening. So moving, she could hardly sit still. If every night could be as diverting as this one, the world would be a better place to live in.

❧

"Mary-Mother-of-God, don't tell me you're dusting books at one A.M. in the morning!"

Myra stares angrily from the top rung. A Jacob's ladder,

leading to a paradise of heavenly treasure. "Please Rose, don't annoy me."

"Since when did you take over the housecleaning? You get down from there right now. Remember your condition."

"I don't want to remember. I only want to find it."

"I know what's coming, Mrs. Russell. After twenty years, you're going to give me the sack. Just the way them buttons replaced that elevator man. Down from there or I'll shake you down like an apple off a tree."

"Rose! Let go. It's my last chance!"

"You want me to phone Dr. Ackerman?"

"Please, he'll only mail me another bill!"

"You want me to tell your son?"

"*Et tu*, Rose!"

"You want everyone to know you been tearing up the house, ripping floorboards, dumping drawers? They'll send you away for sure. And I don't mean on any vacation."

Myra climbs down the shaky steps. "Rose, you mustn't tell a soul. It's a secret. No one in the world knows." A confessional whisper: "Not even me."

Rose looks puzzled.

❧

CAVE GIRL LAUGHS, scream the headlines; CAVE PARENTS PRAY, beam the tabloids. At the year's most important KOOLIE soirée, with the fate of a specie about to be decided, talk focuses on the nine-year-old tot.

"If I were her mother, I'd give her a spanking she'd never forget."

"Absolutely," nods Myra. "Spare the rod and despoil the child. That's what happened to mine."

"Did you read how the President's mobilizing our troops?"

"If only he'd pay more attention to the Bomb business," she frowns, "instead of losing at golf."

"Oh, you must be one of those peace people."

"Yes, indeed," smiles Myra. "SANITY."

"They're the ones with those fancy petitions."

"Not any more." Mrs. Russell appears stern. "Instead of petitions, we're planning a militant Peace Parade."

"How exciting."

"You don't get something for nothing," explains Myra. "Like that search for the Cave Girl. I understand it's costing over half a million dollars a day. Enough to feed an army of orphans for a whole year."

"You're so good on statistics, Mrs. Russell. I don't know how you do it."

"Chess," declares Myra. "It sharpens my faculties. Then too, I attend lectures, go to experimental films and watch educational television. Yes, it's a full life I've had. A very full life."

"You make it sound as if it's all over."

"It's not over till you're buried," she affirms. "And right now, I have no more intention of giving up than the koolie bird."

"Good for you," mutters an ornithologist. "Personally, I think our koolie worries are over. We've sent an expedition into the headwaters of the Nile to trap the last birds. Just a pair, that's all we need. A mateable pair."

"But what if they get together," says Myra, thinking of Paul, "and they don't," thinking of Sybil, "have children?"

"No problem," says the ornithologist. "We've completely doped out the koolie's habits. It's an exact science, this business of reproduction. What koolie birds need when they're mating is to hear the roar of savage animals."

"You're not serious?"

"We've tried it out. It seems that fear provides them with their sex-drive."

"If all they need is fear," says Myra, "just bring them right over. With the Mayor about to demolish the city, the Governor about to bankrupt the state, and the President about to destroy the world, they'll have one grand orgy."

The ornithologist chuckles. Mrs. Russell grabs her pocketbook. Hurry, hurry, an urgent meeting, that explosion of infants, about to bury them in rattles, diapers, and despair.

❧

"CONTROL's image is too broad," declares Vic Brown. "We've got to boil it down to a single wretched family with so darn many kids they have to go to bed hungry and sleep on the floor."

"How dreadful," says Penny Benedikt.

"See! Talk about the human race, and you're bored to death. Mention a few everyday folks, and you're all intrigued. So Brown & Brown will dream up an ideal family with loads of photogenic moppets."

"CONTROL Mother of the Year," says Penny, "an excellent suggestion. When we meet in Washington, the Decoration Committee will announce the winner."

175

"No more than two and one-third children," says Myra. "Enough to replace but not enough to increase."

"What a mind for numbers."

"Isn't she splendid," says Chairman Benedikt. "If only Mrs. Russell would worry more about our immediate problems, coat checking for instance, and not expend so much energy on abstractions."

"What's abstract about population?" cries Myra, indignantly. "My own son has to leave his original Manhattan home, a miniature gem, because he and his wife are taking up too much room. A farmer I know has to leave his farm, in the family since George Washington, because he and his cows use up too much land. Outside the city there's a gorgeous forest with pines, hemlocks, weeping willows—here since pre-history. It all has to be moved now, chopped I mean, because the trees are taking up too much space. So don't call population abstract!"

Smiles of approval. The well-dressed speaker mounts the podium. "In our free and democratic society," she begins.

What a fetching hat. Such vivacious feathers. Goodness, they're from the koolie bird!

". . . over six million acts of love are consummated every single day. Which means, in just our nation alone, a yearly total of over two billion fornications."

Looking at these dignified matriarchs, you'd never guess. But then, it's really the man that does it. The woman simply has to lie back and seem fascinated.

". . . continuing our investigations, we found that pills are too costly; loops, too experimental; diaphragms, too complex; condoms, too unaesthetic; jellies, too ineffectual;

sterilization, too controversial; sponges, too bulky; rhythm, too problematical; withdrawal, too crude; and douches, too unreliable. But, after fifteen years of research, we have got to make a decision. The world can't wait for perfection. It's now or never!"

Myra applauds. The others sit back, quietly exchanging gossip. Of course they're not interested. Frigid, every one of them!

"I think we ought to discuss the cotillion," says Mrs. Benedikt. "We can save the technical know-how for later."

"But this is crucial," protests Myra.

"I move that the research program be postponed for five more years, until we have enough evidence," motions the chairman.

"That's what we voted five years ago," cries the speaker. "For fifteen years we've been putting it off," her plumed hat waving in the oratorical breeze. It *is* a koolie feather, she's positive!

Mrs. Benedikt asks for a show of hands. "The ayes have it. The fifteen-year CONTROL research program is tabled for twenty."

❧

Myra, weary and confused, pauses at the red light, awaiting the glittering green Go-Ahead. Even her insoluble problems can't seem to break the noonday lull. Walking down the same old streets, past the same old stores, rising up in the same old automatic elevator, searching for the same old treasure, terrorized by the same old Rose, bound to poverty by the same old D&K, now 4¼.

CONTROL seems to be just the same old worry, and

war is the same old horror, and chess has the same old trap-mates. Clouds are the same old gray, smog is the same old brown, traffic lights are the same old amber as she traverses, for the ten-thousandth time, the same old Park Avenue.

Movies have the same old love stories. Her heart has the same old imaginary murmur. Her hair is the same old platinum. Her troubles, let's face it, are merely the same old troubles.

Little by little, she's becoming trapped in a relentless rut. Another traffic light. The same old red. She glances at the newspaper headline, the same old . . .

No, different! ARMY IN FINAL RESCUE AT-TEMPT! *Twelve Thousand Troops! Derricks, Drills, Dynamite!*

At last, her mid-noon lull is broken.

～∾

The Tyranny Tests are about to resume. Three billion lulls are about to be shattered. Tanks refuel. Subs dive. Jets soar.

"Debbie, you've got to join. A matter of life or death," screams Myra, frantic and happy, fascinated and troubled.

"War or no war, it's impossible," says Debbie. "If I have to, I'll take Alex and his intravenous into the cellar. But I can't leave him alone for a minute. Not with that awful new nurse. A real sex-pot. Alex says if I discharge her, he'll cut me off without a cent."

"How pathetic."

"I think he's nearing his end."

"Tragic," adds Myra. "The way I look at it, with D&K

178

I've less than a year's supply of money. Not that any of us will last that long."

"You mean," shouts Mrs. Hilliard, "after all my patience, I'll only have a few months to enjoy it!"

"Kovski, my chess master, claims that the Tyranny Tests will escalate into one grand holocaust. Isn't it exciting? I mean, isn't it appalling? I don't know what I mean. All I know is life's full of surprises and I want to take advantage of it. I've got to run! G'bye, Debbie. See you and Alex after the parade. They say there'll be loads of radioactivity. It could mean Alex will get cured. Peaceful uses of atomic energy and all that. Maybe, by next month, he'll be back on his feet. G'bye, again."

An anguished groan from the other end of the phone. Was that Alex? Sounded more like Debbie. But this is no time to start worrying. Hurry, hurry!

❧

"Worthless!" says Tannenbaum. "Our petition was as valuable as a czarist ruble. SANITY's only hope is the Peace Parade."

"A petition with the biggest names in the business," says Vic, looking almost discouraged. "Philosophers, saints, generals. We even scored the classiest signature of them all— the President himself."

"Forget your petitions," advises Kovski, his wrinkles deepening. "I told you, it's hopeless."

"But we can't just give up," objects Myra, looking fretful. What a good time she's having. There's nothing like being socially involved.

179

Kovski produces a reel of tape. "I fed our computer all the data: troop deployments, bomb sites, unemployment figures. It took the Neuron a mere thirty seconds." He holds up the coded conclusion: "Holocaust!"

"Revolting."

"Seven months at most," he adds.

"Incredible!" But it's not incredible. If she sells out now, she'll have just enough money to live a rich and productive seven months. Eight, and she'll be dead broke.

"Even if there isn't a war," warns Kovski, "even if it's only a series of tests, the Neuron XIX says that the atmosphere of our Northern Hemisphere will be like the inside of a garage with the windows bolted and the engines roaring."

Vic Brown glumly mutters slogans, trying to renew SANITY's lost image. He's finally putting two and two together, waking up to how awful the world truly is, about to turn into a realist, like her.

"Infants will be gargoyles. Leukemia, mutations. We'll all be disfigured or decaying or dead."

A shocked silence.

He's wrong, of course. Cockroaches will be completely unharmed. High radiation tolerance. She read it in her latest handbook, *Favorite Fallout Fallacies*.

"According to Neuron, it's all a question of escape. So I put it to work, analyzing the planet's climactic structure —wind patterns, precipitation distribution, cloud cover. Everything pointed to the Southern Hemisphere, where atmospheric radioactivity is a tenth of what we have on this side of the Equator. But that doesn't mean every country down there is safe. A nation like Venezuela is much too close to our Caribbean bases. And areas with high rainfall are out. That narrows the search to one special terrain, a place where it scarcely rains. In other words, a desert."

"What a mind," whispers Myra.

"What's he getting at?" whispers Sid.

"Not only a Southern Hemisphere desert," continues Kovski, "but it also has to be a municipality where, barring a revolution, you can easily obtain the necessities of life— food, shelter and water."

"Rio de Janeiro," beams Myra. Beaches, mountains, Copacabana. A delightful way to spend one's declining years.

Kovski goes on: "Australia and New Zealand are out of the question. Population pressures from Asia are sure to be disastrous. The Kalahari Desert would be ideal, but the blacks are bound to win South Africa, and we, being white, would be exterminated. That leaves only one place, South America."

"I told you!" exclaims Myra. "Rio."

Kovski quotes the computer: " 'A city. On the South American continent. Below Venezuela. In a desert.' Stand by for reply. 5,4,3,2,1,0 . . . 'Nation: Chile. City: Antofagasta. Lat. 23°31′S., Long. 70°20′W. Total rainfall in last one hundred years,' " Kovski clears his throat, " 'Total rainfall: .0000 inches'!"

"But I had my heart set on Rio!"

Vic seems troubled. "Would it look right to run out like rats from a sinking . . ."

"Let's not give up our ship!" interrupts Tannenbaum. "We'll sail the s.s. HOPE into the test zone and protest!"

181

"*S.S. Hope?*" cries Myra. "But that's a hospital ship."

Sid frowns. "Hospital, heck. It's a chartered yacht."

"But it's the same name," says Myra. "I know because I just gave to that cause. A mission of mercy."

"The little lady's got a point," groans Victor. "We'll have to change it."

"Never!" threatens Tannenbaum. "We already christened her."

"We'll look like copycats."

"You should have thought of that before."

Kovski raps for order. "Ladies and Gentlemen, your petition has failed. Your quixotic Peace Parade will fail. And your toy boat will also fail. There's not the slightest statistical possibility for peace. Neither HOPE nor SANITY can stop the inevitable. The only logical defense is to flee into the desert!"

"But our families!"

"Our homes!"

"The treasure! What about the treasure!"

❧

Myra unravels the scrap of paper. Rose O'Connor's nervous scribble: *Goodbye I Have to elope Going South* Of course, Antofagasta! *Take care of yourself Mrs Russell Remember your murmer Sincereley Rose*

Ralph's final bequest, filched from under her nose. While she was debating the fate of the world. At the very moment SANITY was scheming to save the planet. Of all the ingratitude! Why, she must have become completely psychoneurotic. Rose O'Connor, acting out her fantasies, leaping from

182

that narrow cot into a giant matrimonial bed. Rose O'Connor, holding imaginary hands, kissing phantom lips, fleeing to a make-believe desert, paid for by a very real treasure.

Destitute. She'll be forced into a Maisonette cubicle, soon to emerge from the hole that once was STABLES, that hollow in her ransacked hope chest, that gaping cavity which tomorrow could be the Northern Hemisphere. Myra glances at the Happiness brochure with its cheerful Colonials. *Free to the first hundred buyers! Bombproof shelters. Fully stocked with radio, oxygen, and Scotch.*

Bombproof, indeed! An out and out lie. No shelter's deep enough to save them from the latest bomb. She'll have to board the s.s. HOPE with Sid and the others, sail into the test site, stop those tyrannical experiments, halt the holocaust in the nick of time.

She stares at the gap in the encyclopedias, where an empty eye, Ralph's, winks at her lewdly. A missing volume! T for treasure! Of course!

Myra's beggar hands search desperately for something to still her murmurs, her insomnia, her nightmares of global suicide.

Not a pill in the house. "Rose!" she cries, as she tunes in her flickering TV.

Alone, in the darkness of the abandoned apartment, with Rose and her invisible lover fleeing Armageddon, with Debbie praying for a speedy widowhood, with D&K slowly sinking into its ⅜ grave, Myra Russell gazes in full, living color at a televised horror story.

❧

"Damn," says Sid, as the Independence Day Protesters cross the sagging bridge, "take a look at Vic's latest masterpiece."

Myra, her white sneakers bouncing up and down, studies the leaflet: *Peace is good for you. You'll be good for Peace. March on Washington and show them you care.* "But I think it's fine."

"Sure, for namby-pambies. And then that gutless guy has the brass to drive there in his new sports car. Cost him thirty-two thousand Swiss francs."

"But that must be a fortune."

"They say he came into an unexpected inheritance."

Myra and the peace marchers stare glumly at the Hudson, swirling madly below. Polluted with tree trunks and contraceptives. But this is no time to worry about CONSERVE. CONTROL, either.

Why not? What's wrong with constructive worry? She worries about the rain problem, for example. What if the Contrillion dancers bring their umbrellas, where will she put them? The fur coat problem, how to guard them? The hot weather problem, what will she do if no one has anything to check? She'll have to tell the hired girls they're not wanted, hurt their feelings, add to the unemployment problem. Problems, the best way to take your mind off yourself.

There's the koolie problem, that priceless cargo, the last two koolie birds, male and female, due to arrive on the Fourth of July. Everything converging on the same day: the parade, the mating, the ball, the test.

Roadside billboards shout their scurrilous messages. *Buy Insect Doom & Live Comfortable.* CHEMBAN should only see that! *Happiness Suburban Homes—78 Short Miles Ahead*. Well, as they say at DT, you can't stop progress. *Four, Five, Six Bedrooms*. Like so many out-of-CONTROL rabbits!

"I think we're making up," says Tannenbaum.

"What do you mean?" asks Myra, rejoining reality, the world, the Peace Parade.

"My ex-wife and me. Joyce wants to end our separation."

"I'm so happy," letting go of his hand.

"She'll be joining us on the s. s. HOPE. I guess she just got bored, living alone and all that."

"Perfectly understandable," says Myra, grimly.

"The trouble is trying to raise enough money," he groans. "Those chartered ships cost a fortune."

"Yes, money. Life's biggest problem." She feels miserable and she may as well face it. Ever-the-good-sport Myra puts on a resolute smile as he boasts of his ex-wife, his star fundraiser, how beautiful, how vivacious, how serene she is. There's nothing more attractive than what you can't have. Even Ralph, now that he's been gone so long, seems desirable.

"I mean," pouts Tannenbaum, "I can pay *my* share out of a little unexpected windfall . . ."

Myra gasps. "What kind of windfall?"

"Nothing much, really," he grins. "An old bundle of railroad stocks I stumbled onto. Practically worthless."

"What I want to ask you is—where did you stumble? I mean those bonds. I mean . . ."

"We'll sail the HOPE into the test zone and block the whole bloody business," confides Sid.

"Lovely," says Myra, looking distraught. "I mean out on the Pacific, up in the crow's nest, yelling orders to the crew."

"Fight fire with fire," he advises solemnly.

"Fight!" repeats Myra, reflecting how she's afraid to tell the police about Rose, how she's afraid to tell the Welfare Department about her impending destitution, how she's afraid to tell CONSERVE about Paul's Parkland Department bribe, how she's afraid to abandon her plummeting railway, now down to ½ year. "There's nothing," she shouts over the *Battle Hymn of the Republic*, "like a good parade to let off steam."

Igor Kovski gazes at the sky as if searching for missiles. "A penny for your thoughts," frowns Myra. At least *she's* doing something worthwhile, not just dreaming. If only that blister didn't bother her so. And she can hear her insides grumbling like a restless volcano.

They pause at the Leaning Tower of Pizza. Myra orders three: anchovy for Sid, mushroom for Igor and plain, dietetic mozzarella for herself.

"A waste of energy," says Kovski, chewing into the orange triangle. "You'll never get to see the President. And what if you do? When he makes his next move, it'll be checkmate for the whole human race."

"We have to," says Tannenbaum, the anchovies sticking to his teeth. "This way they can't say we didn't try peaceful means."

"You said a mouthful," nods Myra.

"When that Bomb test begins, the only peaceful means," advises Kovski, "will be to clear the hell out. When the

French Revolution started, only the fools hung around. Lost their heads, that's what. When the Nazis came to power the Berlin Jews were so cocky, most of them stayed."

"Foolish them."

"Bars of greasy soap, that's what they turned into. Came the revolution in Austro-Hungary, I grabbed my chessboard and beat it. The others all laughed. 'Kovski, the idiot.' 'Kovski, the turncoat.' But believe me, they're not laughing anymore. Now even the country's been wiped off the map."

"The nerve!"

"And now for the bloodiest revolution of all. Only in this revolution, it isn't people taking over, it's machines, automation, remote control. Well, if the test isn't called off, I'm making the best move on the board, Antofagasta."

"An American refugee," she sighs. "Who would believe it could happen here."

"It hasn't happened yet," says Sid, ordering seconds. "And it won't if our plan goes through."

"The s.s. HOPE?" smiles Kovski.

"Let's go!" shouts Myra. "Hurry, they're ahead of us. They'll think we dropped out. Blister or no blister, I've *got* to get to Washington on time. The Contrillion. I'm on their Checking Committee."

"That's why I admire you," says Sid, as they lick their tomato-stained fingers and continue on their way. "All that energy. How do you ever find the time?"

"I make the time," says Myra. "No, that's not it; I simply have time on my hands, that's how." She glances down at her hands, her blood-red palms. "Hurry!" she cries.

A stagecraft rattle of thunder, doomsday streaks of lightning. "Storm!" shouts Sid.

A shower envelops the six hundred SANITYists. Myra examines her soaked and muddy sneakers. "Sometimes I think Kovski's right. Why not go where it never rains? I mean Antofagasta."

"The important thing is to take a stand," affirms Sid. "Make up your mind and stick to it. Even if it does mean giving up a lousy job."

"Awful," says Myra. "I mean the way you have to be working for her alimony when you should be doing something worthwhile. Look at my husband. Ralphy used to sell plain old dirt, so those things they call apartments could have cement. Of course he made a fortune out of it. But was it worthwhile?"

"At least he left you in the chips."

"Exactly." But it's not exact. Her supply of money, if she dare believe those cryptographic account books, has dwindled to a bare six months.

"Why don't you join us on the s.s. HOPE?" says Tannenbaum, tugging the raincoat away from her onto him.

"Travel," says Myra. "The most enriching experience a human being can have." She tugs back, trying to protect her permanent wave.

"We already have a dozen people signed up," confides Sid. "Secretly, of course."

"Then if *I* went, that would make thirteen. Not that I'm superstitious. I'm really," she explains, "a sort of freethinker. I say whatever comes to my head. And right now, I say what you're doing is positively heroic."

"Gosh, Mrs. Russell, you're the kind we need on our crew. How about it?" A cackle of thunder.

Myra presses against him, fearfully. "I'll think it over," she promises as the two peace lovers huddle in the darkness, exchanging fervent proposals of HOPE.

"Hooray! The buses are here! C'mon gang, on to Washington!"

The grueling three-mile hike is over.

Afraid to push away Sid's groping fingers, afraid to leave the bus for a fattening snack, afraid to look out at the twisting road, Myra falls into a fitful stupor.

She pictures a two-hundred-mile peace trek, growing stronger, bolder, joined by a grateful nation, pouring forth from factories and showrooms, from offices and jailhouses, from potato fields and posh saloons. Earnest secretaries and switchblade juveniles, guitarists and ice-cream vendors, lawyers and bondsmen, the maimed and the deaf, the merely nervous and the totally deranged, heading for the nation's holy shrine, Washington, where the President prepares his catastrophic blessing.

They've got to hurry, stop the Tyranny Tests in time. It's like an old-time movie, with the peace-marching cavalry rushing to protect the mothers and their unborn children from tyrannical redmen. A thrilling spectacular; cast of thousands; a sound track of hymns, folk tunes, marches.

Suddenly, from behind the birch trees, a cordon of dissidents: *Bomb Nowers, Better Deaders,* surrounding the pilgrimage with oaths and taunts.

Love them as thyself! commands Myra in her hateful

189

reverie. As if she should love Paul, that defaulter; or Rose, that sneak thief; or D'Agostino, that traitor; or Fahnstock, that libertine. No, she must forgive and forget, or her mind will overflow with the lurid past instead of a fascinating present.

The procession of six hundred, insistent on a Presidential miracle, winds its way southward. Past auto dumps and tree stumps, past smiling motels and dour cops, past fuming factories and model slums, past whitewashed rockets and blackfaced streetcleaners. Past lines of reporters and peeping-Tom cameras, past incredulous cows and vitriolic parsons, past snapping dogs and displaced rats, ride the brave, the hopeful, the desperate six hundred.

The screech of hysterical brakes. Her nightmare gone, Myra reaches for the emergency pills. Vanished! She examines her face in the compact mirror. Oh, for an untroubled sleep.

She stares at her timepiece, ticking off its Geiger-counter hours, minutes, seconds, transfixed by the fleeting moments. Now it's here, now it's gone. She tunes in to her agitated heart. A murmur above the snores. She'll have to consult her physician. Another sumptuous fee. Another step down the ladder of poverty.

Why fret about war when she should be worrying about her impending penury? Because it's more important, that's why. Because it's more interesting, that's why. Because it helps pass the time of day.

But not the night! Dear God of Technology, without her CHEMBANned pills, not the night.

Myra turns to the East. The cavalcade is greeted by a rain-drenched dawn. Like the feeble light in that newspaper cave. Whatever happened? Probably the poor child was bored to tears. No way out. Nothing but that enticing entranceway. An attempt to find excitement. An attempt to break the lull.

Six hundred dreams are shattered as the convoy of speeding buses pulls to a halt. Twelve hundred shoes resume the grueling march. On to the capitol! Jazz bands take up the beat. Strontium 90 songs, fallout tunes, leukemia ditties. It's all part of the jovial Brown Plan.

Not the Kovski Plan, that exodus into the rainless desert. Not the Tannenbaum Plan, with Noah and his paired-off passengers. But the Victor T. Brown Plan, with music, sandwiches and cheer leaders. Not a bad way to spend a weekend.

Myra joins the unrouged lassies and their unkempt youths, the weighty professors and bony old maids. She lifts her picket to the sky as the guitar-strumming army of peace, trespassing across lawns, dashing through traffic, dodging past catcalls, urinated on by beagles, laughed at by gagsters, harried by policemen, welcomed by grocers, marches on.

"Look," shouts Sid, pointing to a newsstand: TOT TURNS UP! "See, they rescued the cave girl. Twenty thousand troops."

"*Ganz tot,*" snorts Kovski, buying a copy. ARMY MEDICS ATTEMPT REVIVAL. "Leave it to those hypocrites."

"Kind of makes you think," says Myra thinking of her hunger pains, her diet, her health, of war, of peace, of HOPE.

Kovski crumples the newspapers. "Twenty thousand brains and they couldn't dope out a simple labyrinth limited to three dimensions. But then, what can you expect from simpletons? Incidentally, I called in a repair man. The Neuron XIX was a bit deranged. The holocaust is seven months away, not six. A couple of tubes were shot."

Seven months! A whole month past her means. So *let* the Bomb come spinning down. She'll perish even if it doesn't. Better not to think of it.

Kovski grabs her arm. "How about a game of chess to take your mind off things?"

"While we're marching?" Myra looks puzzled. "But we don't even have a set."

"Use the board in your head, Mrs. Russell. Didn't you ever hear of mental chess? Announce your opening."

"It's just that my thoughts are on something else," she explains. "I'm working on a blank verse. Poetry, another fascinating interest of mine. A poem called *I Treasure*. All that's needed is a third word. Pawn to queen four," she mutters absent-mindedly. "I had hoped that you, with your brilliant mind could work it out. If you were a husband and had hidden away your life's savings, how would you tell me in three simple words?"

"First of all, knight to bishop three," says Kovski, commencing his defense. "Second of all, being married to you, Mrs. Russell, I'd rather not think about. Third of all, I'd hide the treasure in a . . ."

"There it is!" shouts an ebullient Sid.

"Where?" cries Myra, tugging at the Chessmaster's lapel.

"Just beyond that monument," beams Tannenbaum.

"Surrender, Mrs. Russell?"

"Never," she cries. "Only where?"

"Then, to continue, knight takes the pawn."

"A disaster," groans Myra, afraid to ask—is it a thirty-cent session or a thirty-dollar lesson?

"Turn down Pennsylvania Avenue!" cries the guide.

"Why don't we do a little sightseeing and finish the game later," says Myra, her mental chess pieces in complete flight.

"Capitulate?" smiles Kovski.

"Never! Only tell me!" She gazes in horror as the battle of the peacemarchers continues: knights unhorsed, bishops defrocked, castles looted, queens raped. Tricked. The Serf Defense has turned into an attack.

"Checkmate!"

"How much," cries Myra, "do I owe you?"

"Thirty," mutters Kovski.

"Cents or dollars?" Myra's heart murmurs an abortive prayer.

"I need the dough," explains Igor. "Antofagasta isn't around the corner, Mrs. Russell. Make it dollars. We'll call it a lesson." He examines her frantic face. "Oh yes, what you were telling me. Perfectly simple. I'd hide it in a Swiss bank of course."

"Swiss bank!" cries Myra. "Why didn't I think of it? An unnumbered Swiss account." She hands him a scrap of paper. "Here's my IOU. I'll redeem it when we get home."

193

"Anyhow, your aptitude for chess was limited," concedes Kovski. "You have an incredible talent, Mrs. Russell, for losing."

Myra and the bedraggled legions pull up to the White House, lower their weary picket signs and demand to see the President.

"Only an hour before the test series," cries Sid, looking desperate.

"Incidentally, I'll settle that thirty dollar IOU for five cash," says Kovski.

"All's fair in love and chess," shrugs Myra, overjoyed at the twenty-five saved. "Here's your five dollars. And here," she rips the promissory note, "is the end of chess. I have more serious things on my mind than games. I've got to rush to Switzerland. To Berne, Lausanne, Lucerne. But first there's the Pacific. The war. We've got to stop it. Only an hour left to convince him."

The plainclothesman returns. "The boss is out to lunch. Georgetown."

The SANITYists dash down the Mall.

"Sorry," says the wine steward. "He's at the Naval Observatory."

Only thirty minutes to go. Up the hill charge the six, now eight hundred.

"Not here," says the chief astronomer. "He's off to . . ."

Only twenty minutes! They've got to reach him, to save the world, the children, the bread, the milk, the future. The angry thousand, with fifteen minutes to go, charge toward the suburbs. Another mob of picketers. Mingling. Confusing.

"Who are they?" demands Myra, trying to shove her way through, with only thirteen minutes and twenty seconds till Hell.

"DIP," cry the signs. "Disease, Impoverishment, Peace."

"C'mon," commands Tannenbaum. "We need all the troops we can muster. Peace, that's exactly what we're for."

"How do you stand on Disease?" asks a gray-haired lady. "What about Impoverishment?"

"Let's not quibble," cries Sid.

"A matter of life or death," shouts Myra. "Naturally we're for Disease. Impoverishment, too."

"In unity there is strength," roars Victor T. Brown, peering out the window of his convertible Mercedes Benz.

The DIPsters, placards on high, attach themselves to the surging band of peace marchers. Joined by pickets against Welfare. Pickets against Race. Pickets against Creed. Pickets against Government. Pickets against Hate. Pickets against Socialism. Pickets against Capitalism. Turbulent pickets. Epileptic pickets. Psychotic pickets. Adjusted pickets. Pickets beyond Belief. Shouting for love, fulfillment, salvation. A hundred worthwhile causes. A thousand fiery slogans. Ten thousand good-doers, united in dissatisfaction. Spinsters and schoolkids, professors and truck drivers, idealists and fatalists. Welded by inhumanity. Bounded by police. Gripped by helplessness. Wracked with anxiety. Trembling with rage.

"Hurry," cries Myra. "Time is running out!"

Twenty thousand irate marchers trap him by the ninth hole.

The President, his game ruined, drops his golf club and

smiles. Reporters sharpen pencils, TV cameras roll in, loud-speakers descend as if from heaven. An enthralled nation listens with bated breath to his carefully modulated voice:

"Dearest friends and countrymen. To those who have marched so long and hoped for too much, I have but one thought. This nation, conceived before God, must not be strangled on the vine of human indifference. Where the tyrant calls for peace, we will answer peace. Where the tyrant calls out halt, we will answer halt. And where the tyrant cries out war, we will answer war. Let them test. Yes, let them. For we of this United and Most Favored Nation have but one reply. It's in black and white, in your revised Constitution. It's in your Bill of Righteousness. Let us learn from these sacred documents what we learned on the frontier, what we learned at Hiroshima, what we learned from Vietnam. That force will be met with force. That bullet will be met with bullet. That test will be met with greater test.

"The State Department informs me that the Tyranny Tests have just begun. You who are so militantly against death, understand that we must proceed without your dissenting vote. For dissension, in these troubled times, is no different from rebellion. And rebellion is not merely unlawful, it is unwarranted. And the Tyranny Tests are not merely unnecessary, they are outrageous. I therefore proclaim," the President raises his index finger as the servicemen draw their revolvers, "the resumption of our own tests, the improved tests, the scientific tests, the clean tests, the Freedom tests!"

"Betrayed!"

"Bastard!"

"Fascinating!"

The stern-faced President picks up his putter. The game continues.

The protesters disperse. To luncheonettes and movie houses, to museums and whore houses, to cocktail lounges and bus terminals. Myra, to the Washington Zoo. The grand unveiling. The very last pair, about to couple, about to save the koolie race from doom.

"A spectacular city," she cries to the harried taxi driver. "All those monuments and memorials. Like Rome. Not that I've ever been there. But someday I plan to."

"Yeah."

"There's nothing like travel to round a person out. Only who has time, now that the world is going to be evaporated."

"Yeah."

"If only there were some way to conserve. I mean the birds. I hope they're happy. Because you can't unless you're happy. I suppose that's why Ralph, my former husband, and I only had one. Paul, a well-intentioned son. His wife, too. After all, it's not her fault. But now it's too late. Everything's going to go. Every leaf, every tree, every building. Isn't that the Washington Monument?"

"Yeah."

"Looks like Cleopatra's Needle. That's in Central Park. An interesting place. Only you don't dare walk there or you'll get clubbed on the head. A ghastly world, shooting all its birds, poisoning its children, contaminating, killing, hating."

"Yeah."

"But we've got to forget all that. If you can't find something worthwhile to think about, you may as well be dead. Quick, taxi, let me out! I've got to see the koolie birds." She hands him a beneficent tip, two hours' worth of life. The sullen cabbie examines the bills. "How do you open this contraption?"

"Two, three . . ." The driver inspects each greenback as if they're counterfeits, like Paul's paper homes, like Sybil's Maisonettes, like her own russet hair, like the Last Forest, now a desolate, graveled plain.

"Members of KOOLIE, at this great unveiling, we dedicate ourselves to the proposition that all species are created equal. That they have certain inalienable rights. That among these are life, children and the right to survive. That the last known pair of koolie birds shall blossom forth into 4, 8 and 16. That they shall become 32, 64, 128. That they shall flourish, prosper and be fruitful, becoming 2048, 4096, 8192 . . ."

Enough! They must CONTROL themselves or there'll be nothing but koolies on every telephone pole, rocket launcher and billboard.

"Future generations will long remember our effort to save an entire species from annihilation. A species which can never be replaced. A species which might have ended its days as stuffed birds in a dusty museum shelf. But because of your splendid cookie drive, this beautiful creature will live on, a memorial to your gallant pastime. Ladies and gentlemen, I give you the last of the koolie birds. Long may they live."

The velvet veil is lifted. A groan of dismay.

"There's only one!"

"Suffocated!"

The ornithologist rushes over. "Good grief," he cries into the anguished microphone. "It's the male. He's dead as a dodo. The race, ladies and gentlemen, is no more!"

"Maybe the female is pregnant."

"Maybe we'll catch another."

"Maybe," cries Myra, "but meanwhile I've got to run!"

"Quick, driver! The Contrillion," handing him the swanky address. "It's starting to rain. We won't have room for the galoshes. I'm ten minutes late. Hurry!"

"You can't rush Father Time, lady."

"I wonder why they call it Father Time. I must look it up. But under 'F' or 'T'? Anyhow, it's more like a woman. Fickle. Close your eyes and it's already night. Wake up and it's suddenly pouring."

"Great for business," he grins, nibbling on a bar of Swiss chocolate.

"What about the children," she cries, "the women and children?"

"Huh?"

"This downpour is as dangerous as death. The Tyranny Fallout is contaminating us all."

"That's just an old wives' tale. Now the Cave Girl, that's fact. Damn shame. But a helluva interesting story."

"Sure it's interesting," concedes Myra. "Only not everything interesting is good. A bored child decides to break her lull by searching for treasure in a complicated cave. And all she discovers is heartache. But if she'd lived, poor thing, she'd have died in a few months, anyhow. Just like the rest of us."

"Wow, look at it pour."

"Radioactive. I can smell it. The whole Northern Hemisphere. Only a few more months."

"A couple more minutes," he mutters. "Don't get impatient."

"The world's about to blow up and you tell me to be patient. The world's about to have more infants than it can feed, and you demand patience. Frankly, I think what happened to the Cave Girl wasn't so bad. With all the children in the world, she'd only have been surplus."

"You ain't got no heart, lady."

"And you don't have any imagination. All you can see is what's in front of you."

"Two dollars seventy cents," says the cabbie, pulling up to the auditorium.

The hall is resplendent with soaring population graphs, silken drapes depicting demographic nightmares, well-designed birth rates, abortion, starvation rates. If only she could have been on the Decoration Committee.

Myra rushes to the booth. "More hangers," she commands her two assistants. "No confusion. Everything must be like clockwork. Number the galoshes," as she holds up two lefts. "No excitement. No mistakes."

A newspaper falls to the floor: CAVE CORPSE BURIED. *Pomp and Splendor Mark Final Rites.* The nine-year-old cadaver, Sybil's unborn infant, lost in a cave-womb, refusing to emerge into a hellish world.

"Keep calm," cries Myra, cramming the headline into a mink stole. "Here they come!"

First the stragglers. Then the rain-drenched hordes. A thousand fashionable dowagers, ten thousand elegant escorts, cavorting about in a modish Dance of Death.

"Never mind the numbers," she barks. "Just hang." Her fingers drip with radioactive droplets. Certain doom. But she's got to forget. Her hands falling off at the wrists, a noble sacrifice, a hopeless cause. "Hurry!"

Mismated overshoes, unnumbered raincoats, stray handbags. She plunges a walking stick into a velvet fedora. Holding a lost umbrella in midair, she hesitates. What's the use? Why fuss over a soaring population when soon they'll need all the people they can muster. Like the koolie birds, just a couple, enough to propagate, enough to continue the future.

If they don't halt the Tyranny Tests—yes, the Freedom Tests, too—the planet will perish even without a war. Right in the midst of its lull, in the midst of armed indifference, in the midst of boredom and wishful thinking.

That's it! That's what counts—HOPE, the ship to arouse this world of miserable wet blankets, to wake them from their lethargy. She'll sell the remains of her stocks. Every single share, now down to ¼. She'll retrieve her loan, every penny Happiness can afford. She'll climb aboard with Tannenbaum and his crew of SANITYists, scouring the shark-infested seas for peace.

"Do your best, girls." Myra flashes her peace badge with its bent sword and mangled plowshare. "Straighten out those coats and boots and galoshes. I've got to run. Zurich, Zermatt, New York. I don't know where I'm going. All I know it's a matter of life and . . ."

～❧

"Alex is deceased," announces Debbie.

"How ghastly!"

"He left me his whole estate."

"Awful," she groans. "That D&K Railroad, I mean. Your estate will be next to worthless. And now you're a widow like me. Positively gruesome."

"I'm heartbroken, of course," smiles Debbie.

"You haven't seen anything," snaps Myra. "Wait till you have to sit alone all day because you don't have any husband. Wait till you have to eat in cheap restaurants by yourself because your husband's vanished. Your money, too. Wait till you have to go to second-run movies because you're too impoverished for firsts. It'll mean making coffee yourself because you can't afford a maid, watching black and white television, because you don't dare splurge on colored. Frankly, with all the trouble it is being a widow, I almost wish poor Ralph were back. And now that Alex is gone, I won't even have a manager for the little that's left. We'll *both* be poor as beggars."

"But Alex left me a fortune."

"What do you mean! I thought he was a firm believer in D&K."

"He was," says Debbie. "But not for himself. *His* money he put into missiles, baby foods and pesticides. The works!"

"Traitor!" shouts Myra, staring at his stiffened corpse. "Warmonger. Population fiend! Pollutioner!"

"His parting words for you were: 'Sell,' " reveals Debbie.
" 'At any price!' As for me, Alex, that little rascal, had a
bagful of tricks up his sleeve. More, my dear, than I ever
dreamed of," glancing at her shining Swiss timepiece. "My
hubby, it seems, came into a totally unexpected . . ."

"Treasure," interrupts Myra. "Right?"

"But I don't want my ego to be too self-centered. After
all, it's you who has the problems. I hate to tell you this,
sweetie, but . . ."

"I want the truth. The bitter truth."

"While you were away on that wild goose chase in Washington, the D&K Railroad took a final plunge. It's completely
bankrupt."

Myra stares out the window at the lethal rain, eating its
way through bricks, stones, souls. "The world," she confides, "is nothing but one terrible trouble."

"*Troubles*," smiles Debbie. "That's it exactly. Maxwell
Fahnstock is going to lead us."

"Debbie Hilliard, what are you talking about?"

"A round-the-globe trip," she explains. "On the s.s. HOPE.
A lovely cruise."

"HOPE!"

"That's right," nods Debbie. "A visit to all the educational
places in the world. The World Literature Tour. Which is
going to be combined with a protest for peace. Which you
know, Myra, is very fashionable these days. Now that I'm
a widow, *I* can afford to be interesting, too."

"Naturally," says Myra, looking away.

"Only I felt rather guilty," confesses Debbie. "I mean
about the D&K affair. So I decided, together with my an-

alyst (what a charmer), to allay my guilt by treating you as a guest to the World Peace & Literature Tour."

"Debbie, you're a miracle."

"And if you feel strange about accepting charity, you can call yourself my traveling secretary."

"Incredible."

"Maxwell could be quite a catch, don't you think?"

"Incredible," she repeats, standing there like a statue, despair permanently chiseled on her granite lips.

"The problem is," says Debbie, "now that poor Alex is finished and I don't have to protect him from those night nurses, I find my days are filled with terrible blank spots."

"Lulls," explains Myra. "You'll get used to them."

"I've tried everything: movies, best-sellers, lectures. Somehow, it's not so exciting when you can go any time you please. Well then, I decided, it must be travel that I need. To kind of round out my personality." She turns on Myra. "What are you standing around for? Let's get moving. We've got to get packed. Passports, injections, luggage, reading matter. Oh, what a busy day. Hurry, there's no time to waste. We've got to hurry, hurry, hurry . . ."

❧

"Now that the railroad is dead, commuters are moving back to the city in droves," says Sybil, looking radiant at last. "Mother, Maisonettes are booming. And maybe we'll have a little surprise for you."

"Bankrupt," whispers Myra, as they skirt the last remaining stable, rotting beneath the poisonous drizzle. "A surprise," she says sadly, looking at the children playing in the streets, in the rain, playing with death, with leukemia, cancer, as if diseases are toys.

Paul whines in her ear. "There's a chance," he goes on, "I'll be able to pay back the loan. Double or nothing. You see, some extra funds suddenly appeared. I mean, I located some missing . . ."

"Cab!" shouts Sybil.

"Treasure," says Myra to herself.

"Actually," Paul climbs into the confession-booth taxi, "I got the idea after talking with you, Mom. But I can't give you any cash right now. You see, our assets have all been frozen. Damn home owners are starting up a lawsuit because their basements are flooded."

"It's because you chopped all the trees," says Myra, her glassy eyes staring at the glistening asphalt.

"Lousy budget sewers," admits Paul. "The company was out of its mind trying to get away with it."

"No roots to hold the moisture," she explains. "Nothing to soak up the radioactive rain."

"Isn't it marvelous, Mother Russell? Once they settle the court cases, you'll be twice as rich as before."

Paul beams. "Happiness Homes has this great new debenture plan. Payable in 1999."

"No more grass," continues Myra. "No bushes. No more streams," she cries. "No more ponds."

"What's she fretting about?"

"Who knows?"

"No more chess," she mutters. "Kovski's fleeing. We've all got to. HOPE! Taxi, we're late. Hurry, hurry!"

"Plenty of time, Mom. Daylight Saving's been repealed. You forgot to set back your watch."

Myra looks at her heirloom timepiece, jeweled like a precious reliquary. Now she'll have to go through it all over again. An extra hour of life. An extra hour killed, wasted, saved. She turns to Sybil.

Is it possible? Her goat's mustache has vanished. She's smiling, contented. Yes, maybe she's pregnant, bearing the future inside her, a grandchild beneath that wrinkle-free dress. "There it is, my ship!" she exclaims, her spirits soaring to a new high.

"God, but it's small," groans Paul, as Mrs. Russell hands the driver an ebullient tip. "Mom, it's nothing but a rusty old scow!"

"It's beautiful," says Myra. "A dream ship."

"It'll never make it," whispers Sybil. "Are you positive she's insured?"

"Bon Voyage," cries Myra, joining Sid at the gangplank with his divorced wife. And Fahnstock, too, holding his mother's stern hand. And Debbie, in gold lamé, trailing behind like a wet blanket. And Kovski, in tailored luxury, gripping an unexpected ivory chessboard. Yes, he's joining them for the Pacific protest. Or will they flee to Antofagasta? No matter, she'll go with them wherever they decide, for better or worse, married to her fate like an indomitable lover. A distant headline. She can barely make it out. Is it possible? CAVE GIRL RESURRECTED! And the ten-year-old genius, grinding away at his camera, recording his *Horrors of Hate, Part IV*. Pictures of people on shore, grinning as they examine the tiny vessel with its leaky repairs and quiltwork patches. It all depends on your point of view. And hers is up on deck, waving back with enthusiasm, with belief, with hope, with fervor. Pago Pago or Geneva, Switzerland, it doesn't matter. Because she can hear Ralph's voice, his fading last words: *I treasure . . . YOU!* That's what he meant. That's the treasure, herself, her own troubled, busy, restless self.

The ship's whistles, bells, toll a fond farewell as they wave to each other, crossing the darkened waters with gay confetti.

"What's she trying to tell us?" shouts Paul.

"What's the matter with her?"

"Maybe," roars Myra from the deck, "don't put it past me, maybe I'll meet someone. A strong and wonderful husband. Maybe we'll sail together into the Bomb Zone, yelling no, stop it! Maybe there'll be peace. Maybe love. Maybe a joyful tomorrow. Maybe I'll just sail on and on as in a movie, a full-color movie with a happy ending. Maybe, all alone, I'll somehow find a future. I'll sail around and around the earth like a lost planet looking for its orbit. Yes, children, that's what I want. An orbit of my own."

"Mom," shouts Paul, from the pier, now an altar, "are you ever coming back?"

A faint voice, a prayer, a dirge, as HOPE's whistles blast forth a *Gloria in Excelsis*, as the crowd chants an anguished Amen, as the longshoremen nod hallelujah, as the city kneels on its dirty knees, as the world, like a pickpocket, fumbles for peace, as Myra, pleading with outstretched arms, cries for the last and uncertain time, "Maybe . . ."